"I'm The Mother. The Legal Birth Mother. I Get To Make The Decisions."

The eyes he'd been admiring only minutes earlier gleamed in a way that caused the hairs on the back of his neck to rise.

"So I have the final say in who will adopt the baby," she continued, "and it won't be an arrogant, unmarried Russian millionaire!"

"Billionaire," he corrected gently, and watched her smolder even as his own anger bubbled.

"The amount of money you have doesn't change a darn thing. She's going to a couple—a family who wants her, who will love her. That's what I intended when I agreed to be a surrogate for Keira, and that's what I still want for her. End of story."

A challenge had been issued. And he fully intended to meet it.

Ruthlessly suppressing his own hot rage, he murmured, "Well then, it seems I'll just have to get married."

It had been worth the temporary flare of temper. Yevgeny watched with supreme satisfaction as Ella's mouth dropped open.

War, Yevgeny suspected, had been declared.

Dear Reader,

Christmas should be a time of hope.

When the year is drawing to a close, but the new year has not yet arrived, Christmas should be the time to spend with family and friends.

But it doesn't always happen that way. And that's the case for Ella, the heroine of *Staking His Claim*, who looks all set to spend Christmas all by herself—yet she hasn't even considered that she will be alone. She's been too busy working to think much about her own happiness.

Then a baby and a tall, dark hero called Yevgeny change everything. And poor Ella faces the hardest choices she's ever had to make.

For Ella and Yevgeny, Christmas becomes a time of hope, new beginnings—and a new life together.

I hope you enjoy Ella and Yevgeny's story as much as I enjoyed piecing it all together.

Merry Christmas!

With love,

Tessa Radley

www.tessaradley.com

P.S. Don't forget to friend me on Facebook!

Staking His Claim
TESSA RADLEY

First published in Great Britain 2013
by Mills & Boon, an imprint of Harlequin (UK) Limited.
Large Print edition 2013
Harlequin (UK) Limited,
Eton House, 18-24 Paradise Road,
Richmond, Surrey TW9 1SR

© Tessa Radley 2012

ISBN: 978 0 263 23784 9

Printed and bound in Great Britain
by CPI Antony Rowe, Chippenham, Wiltshire

TESSA RADLEY

loves traveling, reading and watching the world around her. As a teen, Tessa wanted to be an intrepid foreign correspondent. But after completing a bachelor of arts degree and marrying her sweetheart, she became fascinated by law and ended up studying further and practicing as an attorney in a city firm.

A six-month break spent traveling through Australia with her family rewoke the yen to write. And life as a writer suits her perfectly—traveling and reading count as research, and as for analyzing the world…well, she can think "what if?" all day long. When she's not reading, traveling or thinking about writing, she's spending time with her husband, her two sons or her zany and wonderful friends. You can contact Tessa through her website, www.tessaradley.com

For all my fabulous readers—
it's always wonderful to
write a new book for you!

One

"You've decided to do *what?*"

It was Friday afternoon, the end of a grueling workweek, and Ella McLeod desperately wanted to put up her swollen feet…and relax.

Instead, from the depths of the sofa in her town house living room, Ella bit back the rest of the explosive reaction that threatened to erupt. She hoped wildly that her sister's next words would settle her world back on its axis so that the nasty jolt of shock reverberating through her system might just evaporate.

As if the sight of Ella's swollen belly prodded her conscience, Keira's gaze skittered away and she had the good grace to look discomforted. "Dmitri and I have decided to go to Africa for a year."

Ella shifted to ease the nagging ache in her lower back that had started earlier at the law chambers. Keeping her attention fixed on her sister fidgeting on the opposite end of the sofa, she said, "Yes, I understood that part—you and Dmitri plan to work for an international aid charity."

Her younger sister's gaze crept back, already glimmering with relief. "Oh, Ella, I knew you'd understand! You always do."

Not this time. Clearly Keira thought this was a done deal. It was rapidly becoming clear why Keira had dropped in this evening. And Ella had thought her sister's anticipation about the baby's imminent arrival had driven the surprise visit....

How wrong she'd been!

Gathering herself, Ella said slowly, "I don't quite understand the rest. What about the baby?"

The baby.

The baby in her belly that Keira had been so desperate for. Keira's baby. A baby girl. Keira and Dmitri had been present at the twenty-week ultrasound when the baby's sex had been revealed. Afterward the pair had gone shopping to finish buying furnishings for a nursery suitable for a baby girl.

Yet now that very same baby girl suddenly

appeared to have ceased to be the focus of her sister's universe.

"Well—" Keira wet her lips "—obviously the baby can't come with."

It wasn't obvious at all.

"Why not?" Ella wasn't letting Keira wriggle out of her responsibilities so easily. *Not this time.* This wasn't the course of expensive French lessons Keira had grown tired of...or the fledgling florist business that Ella had sunk money into so that Keira would have a satisfying career when the one she'd chosen had become impossible. This was the *baby* Keira had always dreamed of one day having.

When Keira bit her lip and tears welled up in her eyes, a familiar guilt consumed Ella. Before she could relent—as she always did—she said, "Keira, there's no reason why the baby can't go with you. I'm sure you'll find people in Africa will have babies."

The tears swelled into big, shiny drops. "What if the baby becomes ill? Or dies? Ella, it's not as if this is a five-star beach resort. This is aid work in a poverty-stricken part of Africa."

Refusing to be drawn into her sister's dramatics, Ella leaned forward and tore a tissue from the box on the glass coffee table in front of the sofa, then passed it to Keira.

"Do you even know what kind of infrastructure

exists? You could ask whether a baby would be safe."
But Ella suspected she was fighting a losing battle
when Keira failed to answer. She tried again. "If it's
so unsafe, then what about your own health? Your
safety? Have you and Dmitri thought this through?
Do you really want to be living in a war zone?"

"It's not a war zone," Keira denied hotly. The tears
had miraculously evaporated without a dab from
the tissue that drifted to the carpet. "Credit me with
some sense. It's Malawi. The country is stable—the
people are friendly. It's poverty and illiteracy that
we will be fighting."

So much for Keira's claim that it would be
impossible to take a child there. But Ella knew
she'd lost the battle; Keira had already made up her
mind—the baby was not going with her.

"So what will happen to the baby?"

Silence.

Keira's eyes turned pleading, just like those of
Patches, the beloved spaniel from their childhood.

"No! It is not staying with me." Ella made it a
statement. A *firm* statement. The kind she used
when delivering an ultimatum to opposing counsel.

Keira opened her mouth.

The baby chose that moment to kick.

Ella squeezed her eyes shut and suppressed a gasp

at the hard jab against her ribs. Perspiration pricked at her forehead. She rubbed her side.

Thrusting the pain away, she opened her eyes and said to her sister, "Have you spoken to Jo about your new plans?" Ella suspected Jo Wells, the social worker who had been involved in helping arrange the paperwork side of the adoption for Keira and Dmitri, would be as floored as she was by Keira's change of heart.

"Dmitri is right. We're too young to become parents," Keira said, sidestepping Ella's question. "We haven't even been married a year."

Drawing a deep breath, Ella said slowly, "A bit late to come to the conclusion that you're not ready to be parents."

Nine months too late to be precise.

Ella patted her own swollen stomach and watched mercilessly as Keira flushed.

"This baby is due next week. All your life you wanted to get married, start a family…that's why you did an early childcare course." It was why Ella was now stuck across the sofa from her sister like a stranded whale with a bulging belly. "How can you walk away from your child now?"

She had a nasty suspicion that she knew what—or rather, who—was behind the change of heart. Dmitri's big brother. Yevgeny Volkovoy.

Bossy big brother. Billionaire. Bigot.

Ella couldn't stand the man. He'd been furious to discover that Dmitri had gotten married without his say-so. He'd caused poor Keira endless tears with his terrifying tirades. Only by signing a post-nuptial agreement that allowed Keira the barest of maintenance in the case of divorce, and skewed everything in favor of the Volkovoy dynasty had Keira escaped his ire. Ella'd had a fit when she'd learned about the contract—and her alarm had grown when she read the terms. But by then it had been too late. The marriage was a done deal.

And Keira hadn't asked her for her expertise... or her help.

Of course, Yevgeny hadn't been in favor of the baby plan, either. Ella had known from the moment he'd switched to Russian. Dmitri had gone bright red—clearly he'd been less happy with Big Brother's opinions.

Now it sounded like Big Brother had finally gotten his way and managed to persuade Dmitri that he wasn't ready to become a parent.

Shifting again to ease her body's increasing discomfort, Ella tried to stem the emotions that were swirling around inside her. Disbelief. Confusion. The beginnings of anger. None of this cocktail of emotions could be good for the baby. And, even though Ella had never had any intentions of having her own child, she'd taken great care of this one. She'd eaten well—going to great lengths to cut out her four-cups-a-day coffee habit—she'd even shortened her workday and made certain she'd been in bed by ten o'clock each night. She'd even taught herself to meditate so that the baby wouldn't be contaminated by her stressful workday thoughts.

All because she'd wanted to make sure the baby was perfect. Her gift to Keira.

A gift Keira was now returning. Unborn, rather than unwrapped.

How did one return a baby, for heaven's sake? A baby that was a week away from becoming a live person?

Which brought Ella to...

"You're not leaving for Africa before the baby is born." She made it a statement. "There will be decisions that have to be made before you go."

Panic turned Keira's eyes opaque. "No! I can't."

"What do you mean you *can't?*"

"I can't handle those decisions. We've already booked our tickets. You'll need to make the arrangements."

"Me?" Drawing a deep shuddering breath, Ella went cold. "Keira, this is a baby we're talking about—you can't just walk away."

Her sister's gaze dropped pointedly to Ella's very round stomach. "You're still the legal mother—the adoption doesn't kick in until twelve days after the baby's born. You know that, Ella. Because you told me so yourself."

Of course she knew it. Knowing stuff like that was part of her job as one of the most respected family lawyers in Auckland. But the knowledge was only just starting to sink in that Keira was planning to leave her holding the baby!

"Oh, no!" Shaking her head, Ella said emphatically, "The only reason I lent you my body was so that you could have the baby you always dreamed of having. This is *your* dream, Keira. Your baby." *My nightmare.* Then, in case it hadn't sunk in, she added pointedly, "Yours and Dmitri's."

"It's *your* egg."

"Only because you can't—" Ella bit off the words she'd been about to utter.

Too late.

Keira had gone white.

Driven by remorse, Ella propelled her colossal self from the sofa and reached for Keira. Her sister was as stiff as a wooden block in her arms. "I'm so sorry, sweetheart, I shouldn't have said that."

"It's the truth." Keira's voice was flat. "I don't have eggs or a uterus—I can't have children."

"So why—" Ella almost bit her tongue off. She tightened her hold around her sister.

"Don't worry, you can ask. No, I'll ask for you. 'Why are you doing this? Why are you going to Africa without the baby?' That's what you really want to know, isn't it?"

Ella inclined her head.

"I'm not sure I can explain." Keira shrugged out of her hold.

Given no choice, Ella let her sister go.

While Keira gathered her thoughts, Ella became aware of the stark silence that stretched to the breaking point between them across the length of the sofa. A silent divide. It might as well have been the blue-green of the Indian Ocean that stretched beyond Australia all the way to Africa that yawned between them…because her sister had already retreated mentally farther than the arm's length that separated them.

Then Keira started to speak. "This is something both Dmitri and I have to do." The blank, flat stare she fixed on Ella was a little unnerving. "I have to find myself, Ella. Find out who I am. All my life I wanted to teach little children—and have my own houseful of kids at home." Her eyes grew more bleak. "But things didn't go according to plan."

"Keira—"

"I loved my job at Little Ducks Center—"

"Keira." The pain in her sister's voice was unbearable. "Don't!"

But Keira carried on as if she hadn't heard. "I couldn't work there after the car accident…after I found out the truth—that there never would be any babies."

"Oh, honey—"

Keira ducked away from Ella's enfolding arms.

An unwelcome sense of rejection filled Ella. Followed by emptiness. Instantly she scolded herself for her selfishness. She shouldn't feel hurt. Keira was suffering.

Yet, despite all her empathy for her sister, the most important question still remained unanswered: What about the baby? *The baby I helped create to fulfill your dream?* "But Keira, you will have a baby now—and you have a husband who loves you."

Wasn't that enough?

Eyes softening, Keira admitted, "Yes, I was very, very fortunate to find Dmitri."

Ella hadn't been so sure of that in the beginning. In fact, she'd foreseen nothing but heartbreak ahead for her sister. The arrival of Yevgeny Volkovoy in Auckland had been big news. Not satisfied with inheriting millions from the hotel empire his father had built up, the Russian had expanded the dynasty by building up the best river cruise operation in Russia. In the past few years he'd expanded into ocean cruise liners. With the planned expansion of Auckland's cruise ship terminal, it was not surprising to learn that Yevgeny intended to secure Auckland as a voyage destination. What had been surprising had been learning through the newspapers that the Russian had fallen in love with New Zealand—and planned to relocate himself permanently. He'd sent his brother to New Zealand to secure corporate offices and staff them for Volkovoy Cruising's new base. At first Ella had been less than impressed with the younger Volkovoy. With all the Volkovoy money Dmitri threw around, Ella had considered him spoiled and irresponsible. Nothing fortunate in that. Yet there was no doubt that he loved her sister…and thankfully he'd lost that reckless edge that had worried Ella so much at first. But heading off to Africa without the baby was not the right thing for Keira.

The baby…

Ella's hand crept to her stomach.

Mindful of how much her sister hated it when she nagged, Ella tempered her outrage. "You can't just leave a baby for a few months…or even a year…and hope it will be there when you get back."

"I know that, Ella." Keira's brows drew together.

"Don't try to put the guilts on me. I'm not ready for a baby—neither of us are."

Ignoring her sister's unfair accusation, Ella tried to fathom out what Keira's response meant. Did she intend to give the baby up for adoption? Shock chilled Ella. Had her sister thought this through? She would hate to see Keira suffer when it one day came home to her what she'd lost. Perhaps Keira needed to be reminded of that.

"If you're thinking about giving the baby up for adoption, just remember it's not going to be easy to find a surrogate again if you decide you want a baby when you come back from Africa."

She certainly wouldn't be doing it again. She shouldn't even have done it this time. Dumb. Dumb. Dumb decision. That's what came of making decisions with her heart rather than her head.

Keira flicked back her pale silver hair. "We can do what Yevgeny suggested when we first talked about you being our surrogate—put our names down to adopt a baby."

She'd known Dmitri's high-handed brother was behind this!

The ache in her lower back that had been worsening all day, intensified. It wasn't worth arguing with Keira, pointing out that putting down your name didn't guarantee a baby because so few became available for adoption. And when one did, the legal mother had the final say. She alone could choose whichever couple she wanted—there was no waiting list, no way to predict who she would choose.

But right now Keira's future plans were not her concern.

"And what about this baby?" Ella knew she sounded angry. But, damn it, she *was* angry. Yevgeny made her blood bubble—even when he wasn't present. Just the mention of the man was enough! "You can't just dump it—"

"I'm not dumping it— You're the legal mother. I know you'll make the best decision for the baby." There was an imploring expression in her sister's eyes that caused the hairs at the back of Ella's neck to stand on end.

Oh, no! Keira *had* planned to leave the baby with her and come back to claim it. Panic prickled through her. "I *can't* keep the baby."

Keira's eyes teared up again. "I know I shouldn't have expected you to. But you always wanted the adoption of the baby to us to be an open one. So I hoped you would consider…"

"No!" Panic swamped Ella. "We have a surrogacy arrangement—"

Keira was shaking her head. "But Ella, you explained we can't actually adopt the baby until after you sign the consent to give her up on the twelfth day. As the legal mother, you're entitled to change your mind—but so are we."

She'd explained the legalities too well to her sister. Ella swallowed a curse. "You can't change your mind—because I can't keep this baby."

A wave of sick helplessness engulfed her.

Keira sighed. "We already have. We're not ready to raise a child. I don't even want to think about the decision you're going to have to make, but you have to do what you feel is right, Ella. It's your body, your b—"

"Don't tell me it's my baby!"

Keira looked doleful. "I think I always knew deep in my heart that you wouldn't agree to keep her, and I've made peace with that. Even though I had so hoped…" Her little sister's voice trailed away.

Dear God.

Did Keira not know how much this *hurt?* What she was asking? The pain that pierced her chest was sharp and unforgiving. And guilt made it worse. Ella wished she could burst into tears…weep and wail. But she couldn't. Instead, she fought for composure.

She'd always been the adult in their relationship. No doubt Keira had known all along she would agree to sort everything out.

Her heart was racing, and her head had started to

pound. The ache in her back seemed to be growing worse by the minute. Ella knew all this couldn't be good for the baby. She had to calm down. *Think of the baby.* She drew a shuddering breath…counted to five…and exhaled slowly.

Pulling a cloak of assumed indifference around herself, Ella said with every bit of dignity she could muster, "I have a job—a demanding job. I don't have time for a pet, much less a baby." Ella would've loved a pet—a cat. But she didn't have time to care for any living thing.

Keira was staring at her again, her bottom lip quivering.

Ella refused to feel one bit guilty. She was *not* going to be left holding the baby; she couldn't keep it. That had never been the plan. The baby had been conceived for Keira—and Dmitri—to parent. This was not her baby.

Lifting her hand from her belly, she said, "Then we're in agreement. I have no choice but to give your baby up for adoption."

"If you see no other way out."

Before she could reiterate that this was not her preference, that the baby was Keira and Dmitri's responsibility, to her horror Ella felt the warm, wet flood as her water broke.

Keira's baby girl was not going to wait another week to be born.

* * *

Night had already fallen by the time Yevgeny Volkovoy strode into the waiting room set aside for family visitors on the hospital's first floor. He didn't notice the calming decor in gentle blues and creams lit up by strategically placed wall sconces, or even the soft-focus photographs of Madonna-like mothers cradling babies that hung on the wall. Instead, his focus homed in on where his brother sprawled across an overstuffed chair while watching a widescreen television.

Fixing startlingly light blue eyes on Dmitri, he demanded, "Where is he?"

"Who?" Dmitri swung a blank look up at him.

"The child."

"It's not a boy...it's a girl," his brother corrected him even as the soccer game on the television recaptured his attention. "I told you that after the ultrasound."

Yevgeny suppressed the surge of bitter disappointment. He'd been so sure that the ultrasound had been read wrong. He should've known! For almost a century his family had produced boys...there hadn't been a girl in sight. How typical of Ella McLeod to give birth to a girl. Contrary creature.

He waved a dismissive hand. "Whatever. I want to see her."

Retracing his steps out of the family room he emerged in time to see his sister-in-law appear through the next door down the carpeted corridor. Yevgeny strode forward. Nodding at his startled sister-in-law as he passed her, he entered the private ward beyond.

Keira's icicle sister was sitting up in the bed, propped up against large cushions.

Yevgeny came to an abrupt stop. He had never seen Ella McLeod in bed before.

The sight caused a shock of discomfort to course through him. Despite the fact that she barely reached his shoulder when she was on her feet, she'd always seemed so formidable. Stern. Businesslike. Unsmiling. Even at family occasions she dressed in a sharp, formal fashion. Dark colors—mostly black dresses with neck scarves in muted shades.

Now he allowed his gaze to drift over her and take in the other differences.

No scarf. No oversize glasses. No makeup. Some sort of ivory frilly lace spilled around the top of her breasts. She looked younger…paler…more fragile than he'd ever seen her.

The icicle must be thawing.

Yevgeny shook off the absurd notion.

As though sensing his presence, she glanced up from the screen of a slim white phone she'd been squinting at. Antagonism snaked down his spine as their eyes clashed.

"What are you doing here?" she demanded.

"Where is the baby?"

He'd expected to find the child in her arms.

He should've known better. There wasn't a maternal bone in Ella McLeod's frozen body. No softness. No tender feelings. Only sharp, legal-eagle eyes that she usually disguised with a pair of glasses—and from all accounts, a steel-trap brain. According to the rumor mill her law practice did very well. No doubt her success came from divorce dollars siphoned off men with avaricious ex-wives.

Ella hadn't answered. A haunted flicker in her eye captured his attention, but then the fleeting expression vanished and her focus shifted beyond him. Wheeling about, Yevgeny spotted the crib.

Two strides and he stood beside it. The baby lay inside, snugly swaddled and fast asleep. One tiny hand curled beside her cheek, the fingers perfectly formed. Her lashes were impossibly long, forming dark curves against plump cheeks. Yevgeny's heart contracted and an unexpected, fierce rush of emotion swept him.

It took only an instant for him to fall deeply, utterly irrevocably in love.

"She's perfect," he breathed, his gaze taking

in every last detail. The thatch of dark hair—the Volkovoy genes. The red bow of her pursed mouth.

A smile tilted the corners of his mouth up.

Reaching out, he gently touched the curve where chin became cheek with his index finger.

"Don't wake her!"

The strident demand broke the mood. Turning his head, Yevgeny narrowed his gaze and pinned the woman in the bed.

"I had no intention of waking her," he said softly, careful not to disturb the infant.

"It's only a matter of time before she wakens with you hovering over her like that."

"I never hover." But he moved away from the cot—and closer to the bed.

Ella didn't respond. But he'd seen that look in her eyes before. She wasn't bothering to argue… not because she'd been swayed by his denial, but because she was so damn certain of the rightness of her own opinion.

The woman was a pain in the ass.

The polar opposite of her sister, she was the least motherly woman he'd ever encountered—with the single exception of his own mother.

Maybe it was as well she wasn't cradling the baby; she'd freeze the little bundle if she got close enough.

Ella was ice to the core—he'd been mistaken to imagine a thaw.

"Dmitri called to tell me you're planning to give up the child for adoption?" No discussion. No consultation. She'd made a life-changing decision that affected all of them, by herself. It was typical of the woman's arrogant selfishness.

"Then you must've heard that your brother and my sister have decided not to adopt the baby."

Was that irony buried in her voice? He couldn't read her expression. "Yes—Dmitri told me at the office."

"At the same time that Keira was visiting me."

This time he definitely detected an edge. But he was less concerned about her annoyance than discovering the fate of the oblivious newborn in the cot. "So it's true? You intend to give up the baby just like that?"

Her chin shot up three notches at the snapping sound his fingers made. "I will take care of the arrangements to find a new set of parents as soon as I can." Ella glanced down at the phone in her lap, then back at Yevgeny. "I've already left a message for the social worker who's handling the adoption proceedings for Keira and Dmitri, notifying her of their change of mind and requesting that she get in touch with me ASAP."

"Of course you have." It certainly hadn't taken

her long to start the process to get rid of the baby. Anger sizzled inside him. "You never considered keeping her?" Not that he'd ever allow the child to stay in her care.

She shook her head, and the hair shrouding her face shimmered like the moonlit wisps of cloud outside the window. "Not an option."

"Of course it isn't."

She stared back at him, managing to look haughty and removed in the hospital bed. So certain of the rightness of her stance. "Identifying suitable adoptive parents from Jo Wells's records is the only feasible option."

"'Feasible option?'" Was this how his own mother had reasoned when she'd divorced his father and lied her way into sole custody, only to turn around and abandon the same sons she'd fought so hard to keep from their father? "This is a baby we're talking about—you're not at work now."

"I'm well aware of that. And my main concern now is the best interests of the child—exactly as it would be if I was at work."

Yevgeny snorted. "You're a divorce lawyer—"

"A family lawyer," she corrected him. "Marriage dissolution is only a part of my practice. Looking after the best interests of the children and—"

"Whatever." He waved an impatient hand. "I'd

hoped for a little less *business* and a little more emotion right now."

From the lofty position of the hospital bed she raised an eyebrow in a way that instantly rankled. "You don't transfer skills learned from business to your home life?"

"I show a little more compassion when I make decisions that relate to the well-being of my family."

She laughed—a disbelieving sound. Yevgeny gritted his teeth and refused to respond. Okay, so he had a reputation—well-deserved, he conceded silently—for being ruthless in business. But that was irrelevant in this context. He'd always been fiercely protective of those closest to him. His brother. His father. His *babushka.*

He studied Ella's face. The straight nose, the lack of amusement in her light brown eyes—despite her laughing mouth. No, he wasn't going to reach her—he doubted she had any warmth to which he could appeal.

Giving a sharp, impatient sigh, he said, "You've got blinkered vision. You haven't considered all the *feasible* options."

For the first time emotion cracked the ice. "I can't keep the baby!"

Two

Ella's desperation was followed by a strained silence during which Yevgeny looked down his perfectly straight nose at her. Something withered inside her but Ella held his gaze, refusing to reveal the fragile grief that lingered deep in her most secret heart.

But she wasn't going to keep the baby.

And she'd hold firm on that.

For her sanity.

Finally he shook his head. "That poor baby is very fortunate that you will not be her mother."

The contempt caused Ella to bristle. "I agreed to be a surrogate—not a mother."

"Right now you're the only mother that baby has—you're the legal mother."

God.

This was never supposed to have happened. She stuck her hands under the bedcovers and rested them on the unfamiliar flatness of her belly. After so many months of having a mound, it felt so odd. Empty.

And, with the baby no longer moving inside, so dead.

Why had she ever offered to donate her eggs—and lend her womb—to create the baby her sister had so desperately wanted?

The answer was simple. She loved her sister...she couldn't bear to see Keira suffer.

Ah, damn. The road to hell was paved with good intentions. Now look where it had landed her—in an entanglement that was anything but simple. Ella knew that if she wasn't careful, the situation had the potential to cause her more pain...more hurt... than any she'd ever experienced before. The only way through the turbulent situation was to keep her emotional distance from the baby—not to allow herself to form that miraculous mother-baby bond that was so tenuous, yet had the strength of steel.

But there was no need to offer any explanation to the insensitive brute who towered over the hospital bed.

Rubbing her hand over her strangely flat stomach,

Ella pursed her lips. "I'm well aware that I'm her legal mother."

Mother. Just one word and her heart started to bump roughly. She couldn't keep the baby. *She couldn't.*

Carefully, deliberately she reiterated, "It was never the plan for me to remain her mother. This. Is. Not. My. Baby."

It felt better to spell it out so firmly.

The surrogate agreement had been signed, the adoption proceedings had been started. All that needed to happen to formalize the situation had been to get through the twelve-day cooling-off period the New Zealand adoption laws provided. Once that period had passed, and the mother was still sure she wanted to give up the baby, the adoption could go ahead. But Ella had never contemplated reneging on the promise she'd made to her sister. And she'd certainly never expected Keira to be the one to back out!

"She was created for your brother and my sister— to satisfy their desire for a family. By assisting with her conception and bringing her into the world I've kept my part of the agreement." Damn Keira and Dmitri. "In fact, I've gone way beyond what was expected of me."

His mouth slanted down. "That is your opinion."

"And I'm entitled to it." Ella drew a steadying breath, felt her stomach rise under her hands, then calmness spread through her as she slowly exhaled. "You shouldn't expect me to even consider keeping the baby. Keira and Dmitri changed their minds about becoming parents—not me." She'd had enough of being blamed for something that wasn't her fault. And she was furious with Keira, and Dmitri, for landing her in this predicament—probably because the man standing beside the bed had caused it with his initial resistance to the baby in the first place.

But before she could confront him with his responsibility for this mess, he was speaking again, in that staccato rattle that hurt her head. "Stop making excuses. It tells me a lot about the kind of person you are—that even in these circumstances you can abandon the baby you've carried for nine months…the baby you've just given birth to."

What was the man's problem? Hadn't he listened to one word of what she'd been saying? She drew a shuddering breath. "Let's get this straight. Regardless of the position in law, this is Keira's baby, not mine." Where was her sister? She'd landed Ella in this mess, now Keira had disappeared. She'd been here a few minutes ago, but now Ella couldn't even hear her voice in the family room next door. The loneliness that seared her was as unexpected as it was alien.

For once in her life, she could do with her younger sister's moral support. But of course, that was too much to expect. "I *never* intended to have children."

"Never?"

"That's right. Never." Under the bedcovers she clenched her hands into fists.

He shook his head and this time the look he gave her caused Ella to see red.

"And what about your precious brother?" It burst from her. "What about his part in this? He's the baby's biological father. Why don't you harangue him about his responsibilities? Why pick on me?"

For the first time, his glance slid away. "This has nothing to do with my brother."

Her anger soared at the double standard. "Of course not. He's male. He gets to donate his seed and walk away scot-free from all responsibility. It's the woman who carries the baby—and the blame, right?"

Yevgeny shot her a strangely savage look. "I'm not discussing this any further. I will absolve you from all blame and responsibility—*I* will adopt the baby."

"She will become my responsibility," continued Yevgeny, rather enjoying seeing cool, icy Ella looking uncharacteristically shaken. "And *I* do take care of my responsibilities."

Her mouth opened and closed, but no sound came out. Yevgeny's pleasure grew. How satisfying to discover that the always eloquent Icicle Ella, like other mere mortals, could suffer from loss of words.

"You…you live in a penthouse. Y…you're not married…" she finally stuttered out. "A baby ought to be adopted by a couple who will care for it."

It was a great pity she couldn't have remained speechless for a while longer.

"I can buy a house." Yevgeny was determined to ignore the jab about a wife. "And the baby is not an it," he rebuked gently.

Her brown eyes were wide, dazed. "What?"

"You said the baby should go to a couple who love *it*—she's not an it."

"Oh." A flush crept along her cheeks. "Of course she isn't. I'm sorry."

It was the first time he'd ever heard Ella McLeod apologize…and admit she was in the wrong. Yevgeny refused to acknowledge even to himself that he was secretly impressed. Or that it made him feel a little bit guilty about enjoying her confusion.

He studied her. To be truthful her eyes were luminous. Gold-brown with a hint of smoke. Like smoky honey. And the flush gave her pale cheeks a peachy warmth he'd never noticed before. She looked almost pretty—in an ethereal, fragile way that did not normally appeal to him.

In the spirit of reconciliation he felt compelled to add, "And I will care for her."

"A procession of big-bosomed careworkers is not what I had in mind."

Reconciliation was clearly not what Ella had in mind. He suppressed a knowing smirk at how quickly the fragile act had lasted and gave in to the urge to provoke her. "You have something against motherly, homely women?"

The look she gave him would've frozen the devil at fifty feet. "I wouldn't describe a Playboy centerfold model as homely."

This time he allowed himself to smile—but without humor. "I will need some help with the baby...but you may rest assured the criteria for hiring her caregivers will not be physical attributes. I will make sure that the women I employ will be capable of providing her—" he glanced at the baby and realized he didn't yet know her name "—with all the womanly affection the infant will require."

"You will need a wife."

Yevgeny forced a roar of laughter as Ella repeated the ridiculous suggestion. "The child will have far more than a young, struggling couple could ever give her—I don't need a wife to provide it."

"I'm not joking." Ella pressed her lips together. "And I'm not talking about the possessions you can give her—I'm sure you could provide a diamond-encrusted teething ring. But she deserves to have two parents who love her unreservedly."

His laughter ceased. "You're living in a dream if you think that happens simply because a child has two parents." His own mother was living proof of that. To ease the turmoil that memories of his mother always brought, Yevgeny stretched lazily, flexing his shoulders. He noticed how Ella looked away. "She will have to make do with me alone."

That brought her eyes back to him. "Forget it. It's not going to happen—I won't let it."

"It's not only your decision. Fathers have rights, too." He lifted his lips in a feral, not-very-amused grin. "I'm stepping into my brother's shoes."

"As you pointed out, I'm the mother. The legal birth mother." Did she think he'd missed her point? Yevgeny wondered. "I get to make the decisions," she was saying now. "I need only to consider the best interests of the child."

The look on her face made it clear that his solution was not what she considered in "the best interests of the child."

He froze as he absorbed what she was getting

at. "How can that be true? This is the twenty-first century!"

"Quite correct. And a child is no longer a chattel of the head of the household."

The eyes he'd been admiring only minutes earlier gleamed in a way that caused his hackles to rise.

"So I have the final say in who will adopt the baby," she continued, "and it won't be an arrogant, unmarried Russian millionaire!"

"Billionaire," he corrected pointedly and watched her smolder even as his own anger bubbled.

"The amount of money you have doesn't change a darn thing. She's going to a couple—a family who wants her, who will love her. That's what I intended when I agreed to be a surrogate for Keira, and that's what I still want for her— I'll make sure the adoption agency is aware of that requirement. You're not married—and you're not getting the baby. End of story."

Her bright eyes glittered back at him with the frosty glare of newly minted gold.

A challenge had been issued. And he fully intended to meet it.

Ruthlessly suppressing his own hot rage, he murmured, "Well, then, it seems I'll just have to get married."

Yevgeny watched with supreme satisfaction as Ella's mouth dropped open.

War, Yevgeny suspected, had been declared.

Ella did a double take. "You? Get married? So that you can adopt a child?"

She hadn't thought Big Brother Yevgeny could surprise her. She'd thought she had his number. Russian. Raffish. Ruthless. But this announcement left her reeling. What would this playboy Russian billionaire want with a child, a *girl* child at that?

Which led her to say, "But you don't even want a girl."

Something—it couldn't be surprise—sparked in the depths of those light eyes. "What made you think that?"

"I heard you…" Ella thought back to that moment of tension when she'd heard his voice in the family room next door.

"When?"

"As you came in." She searched to remember exactly what he'd said. Slowly she said, "You asked where the *boy* was. You never even considered that the baby might be a girl."

"Aah." He smiled, a feral baring of teeth. "So *obviously* that meant I wouldn't welcome a girl, hmm?"

Sensing mockery, Ella frowned. "Why would you

want a child? Any child?" Wasn't that going a little far—even for Yevgeny—to get his own way?

Yevgeny shrugged. "Perhaps it is time," he said simply.

"For a trophy toddler?"

"No, not a trophy."

"Not like your girlfriends?"

That dangerous smile widened, but his eyes crinkled with what appeared to be real amusement. "You yearn to be one of my trophies?" he asked softly—twisting her insides into pretzels.

An image of his latest woman leaped into Ella's mind. Nadiya. One of a breed of supermodels identified by their first names alone. Ella didn't need a surname to conjure up Nadiya's lean body and perfect face that were regularly featured in the double-page spreads of glossy fashion magazines. Barely twenty, Nadiya was already raking in millions as a face for a French perfume, which she wore in copious amounts that wafted about her in soft clouds. Six foot tall. Brunette. Beautiful. With slanting, catlike green eyes, which devoured Yevgeny as though he were a bowl of cream. Enormously desired by every red-blooded man on earth. A trophy any man would be proud to show off. So why should Ella imagine Yevgeny would be any different?

"That's a stupid question," she said dismissively.

"Is it?"

"Of course, I don't want to be any man's trophy." Ella was not about to be dragged into the teasing games he played. She gave him a cool look— mirroring the one she'd caught him giving her earlier—and let her eyes travel all the way down the length of his body before lifting them dismissively back to his face. "Anyway, you're not the kind of man I would ever date."

He was laughing openly now. "That's not an insult. From my observation, there is *no* kind of man you date."

The very idea that he'd been watching her, noting her lack of romantic attachments, caused a frisson to run along her spine. She refused to examine her unease further, and focused back on the bombshell he'd delivered. "You can't adopt this baby."

He came another step closer to the bed. "Why not?"

"I've already told you. You're not married."

"That's old-fashioned." He leaned over her. "Ella, I never expected such traditionalism from you."

His closeness was claustrophobic. He was so damn big. "Everyone knows you're a workaholic—you're never home." Yevgeny had less time for a kitten than she did.

At that, he thrust out his roughly stubbled chin. "I'll make time."

Right.

Somewhere between his twenty-hour workday and his even more hectic X-rated nightlife? The man obviously never slept—he didn't even take time to shave. His life was littered with women— even before his latest affair with Nadiya, she'd seen the pictures in the tabloids. Keira and Dmitri remained fiercely loyal and insisted the news was all exaggerated but Ella ignored their protests. They'd been brainwashed by the man himself. Ella knew his type—she'd seen it before. Powerful men who treated women like playthings. Men who kept their women at home, manacled by domesticity and diamonds, before stripping them of everything— including their self-respect—when the next fancy caught their eye.

"Sure you will."

"Damn right I'll take care of her."

As if the baby felt his insistence, she made a mewing noise and stirred. The pretzel knot in Ella's stomach tightened, yet thankfully the baby didn't wake. But at least it got rid of Yevgeny—he'd shot across to the cot and was staring down into the depths.

Ella breathed a little easier.

"Money doesn't equal care." She flung the words at the back of his dark head.

At her comment, his dark head turned. Ella resisted the urge to squirm under those unfathomable eyes.

"What's her name?"

"She doesn't have one." Ella had no intention of picking out a name—that would be a fast track to hell. Attachment to the baby was a dark and lonely place she had no wish to visit.

"Keira didn't choose one?"

"Not a final name."

It had puzzled Ella, too. Keira had spent weeks pouring over books, searching websites for inspiration. But she'd never even drawn up a short list. Now Ella knew why: Keira had been dithering about motherhood. Choosing a name would've been a tie to bind her to the baby.

To rid herself of that critical, disturbing gaze, Ella said, "I can ask Keira if there's one she particularly liked."

Yevgeny's gaze didn't relent. "You were supposed to be the baby's godmother, yet you have no idea of the names your sister might have been considering?"

She was not about to air her theory about why Keira hadn't picked a name in order to jump to her own defense. She simply stared back at him wordlessly and wished that he would take his big intimidating body, his hostile pale blue eyes and leave.

"Why don't you ask Dmitri what they planned to name the baby?" Let him go bully his brother. Ella had had enough. "Anyway, the baby's new parents will probably want to pick one out. Now, if you don't mind, it's been a long day. I'm tired, I need to rest."

The baby chose that moment to wake up.

At the low, growling cry, Yevgeny scooped her up in his arms and came toward the bed.

No. Panic overtook Ella. "Call the nurse!"

"What?"

"The baby will be hungry. Call the nurse to bring a bottle—they will feed her."

He halted. "The *nurses* will feed her? From a bottle?"

Ella swallowed. "Yes."

Disbelief glittered for an instant in his eyes, then they iced over with dislike. He thrust the waking baby at her. "Well, you can damn well hold her while I go and summon a nurse to do the job that should be yours."

"She's not my baby..." Ella's voice trailed away as he stalked out of the private ward leaving her with the infant in her arms.

Three

The baby let out a wail.

Ella stared down at the crumpled face of the tiny human in her arms and tried not to ache.

How dare Keira—and Dmitri—do this to her?

She'd barely gotten her emotions back under control when, a minute later, Yevgeny swept back into the ward with the force of an unleashed hurricane. Ella almost wilted in the face of all that turbulent energy. In his wake trailed two nurses, both wearing bemused, besotted expressions.

Did he have this effect on every woman he encountered?

No wonder the man was spoiled stupid.

At the sight of the baby in her arms, the nurses

exchanged glances. Ella looked from one to the other. The baby wailed more loudly.

"Feed her," Yevgeny barked out.

Instead of rebuking him for his impatience, the shorter nurse, whom Ella recognized from the first feed after the baby's birth, scurried across to scoop the baby out of her arms, while the other turned to the unit in the corner of the room and started to prepare a bottle in a more leisurely fashion. Freed from the warm weight of the baby, Ella let out a sigh of silent relief…and closed her eyes.

They would take the baby to the nursery and feed her there. Ella knew the drill. All she needed to do was get rid of Yevgeny, then she could relax…even sleep…and build up the mental reserves she would need for when the baby returned.

"Do you want the bed back raised higher?"

That harsh staccato voice caused her eyelashes to lift. "If you'll excuse me, I plan to rest."

"No time for rest now." He gestured to the nurse holding the bundle. "You have a baby to feed."

Ella's throat tightened with dread.

"No!" Ella stuck her hands beneath the covers. She was not holding the baby again, not feeling the warm, unexpected heaviness of that little human against her heart. "I am not nursing her. She will be bottle-fed. The staff is aware of the arrangement—we've discussed it."

The nurse holding the baby was already heading for the door. "That's right, sir, we know Ms. McLeod's wishes." The other nurse followed, leaving Ella alone in the ward with the man she least wanted to spend time with.

Yevgeny opened his mouth to deliver a blistering lecture about selfish, self-centered mothers but the sound of light footsteps gave him pause. Ella's gaze switched past him to the doorway of the ward.

"Can I come in?"

The tentative voice of his sister-in-law from behind him had an astonishing effect on the woman in the bed. The tight, masklike face softened. Then her face lit up into a sweet smile—the kind of smile she'd never directed at him.

"Keira, of course you may." Ella patted the bedcover. "Come sit over here."

Yevgeny still harbored resentment toward his brother for the shocking about-face on the baby—not that he'd ever admit that to Ella—and he found it confounding to witness her warmth to her sister. He'd expected icy sulks—or at the very least, reproach. Not the concern and fondness that turned her brown eyes to burnished gold.

So Ella was capable of love and devotion—just not toward her baby.

Something hot and hurtful twisted deep inside him, tearing open scars on wounds he'd considered long forgotten.

To hide his reaction, he walked to the bed stand where a water pitcher sat on a tray. Taking a moment to compose himself, he poured a glass of water then turned back to the bed.

"Would you like some water? You must be thirsty."

Surprise lit up Ella's face.

But before she could respond, a vibrating hum sounded.

"That will be Jo Wells. I left an urgent message for her earlier." Ella's hands dived beneath the covers and retrieved her phone.

In the midst of perching herself on the edge of the bed, Keira went still.

And Yevgeny discovered that he'd tensed, too. Given Ella's reluctance to keep the child, she should've been grateful for his offer to take the baby. She could wash her hands of the infant. He'd never contemplated for a second that Ella would actually turn him down.

Her insistence on getting in touch with the social worker showed how determined she was to see through her plan to adopt the baby out. Evidently she wanted to make sure it was airtight.

The glass thudded on the bed stand as he set it down, the water threatening to spill over the lip. Yevgeny didn't notice. He was watching Ella's brow crease as she stared at the caller ID display.

"No, it's not Jo—it's my assistant," she said.

The call didn't last long. He glanced at his watch—7:00 p.m. on a Friday night. She'd be charging overtime rates. Ella's tone had become clipped, her responses revealing little. Another poor bastard was about to be taken to the cleaners.

Ella was already ending the call. "If you wouldn't mind setting up an appointment for early next week I'd appreciate that," she murmured into the sleek, white phone. "Just confirm the time with me first, please."

That caught his attention.

As soon as she'd killed the call, he echoed, "Early next week? You're not intending to go back to work that soon. Have you already forgotten that you have a newborn that needs attention?"

"Hardly." Her teeth snapped together. "But I have a practice to run."

"And a newborn baby to take care of."

"The baby wasn't supposed to arrive for another week!" Ella objected.

Keira laughed. "You can't really have expected a baby to conform to your schedule, Ella. Although, if you think about it, the baby did arrive on a Friday evening. Maybe you do already have her trained."

Ella slanted her sister a killing look.

It sank in that Ella *had* expected the baby to conform. Clearly, she rigorously ran her life by her calendar. Why shouldn't a baby comply, too? Yevgeny started to understand why Ella could be so insistent that she'd never have a baby.

Her selfishness wouldn't allow for it.

The woman never dated. She didn't even appear to have a social life—apart from her sister. Keeping the baby would mean disruption in her life by another person. Ella was not about to allow that. Everything he knew about her added up to one conclusion: Ella was the most self-centered woman he'd ever met.

Except there was one thing wrong with that picture…

Keira must have begged to get her sister to agree to be a surrogate in the first place. Ella carrying the baby for nine months was the one thing that went against the picture he'd built in his mind. Allowing her body to be taken over by a baby she had no interest in was a huge commitment.

But Yevgeny knew even that could be explained— Ella was a lawyer. She knew every pitfall. And she was such a control freak she wouldn't have wanted to risk some other surrogate changing her mind once the baby was born. This way she could make sure that Keira got the baby she and his brother had planned.

Ella was speaking again. He put aside the puzzle of Ella's motivations and concentrated on what she was saying. "Well, that's when I planned my maternity leave to begin," she was informing Keira. "Another week and everything in the office would've been totally wrapped up—I planned it that way."

"Oh, Ella!" The mirth had faded from his sister-in-law's face. "Sometimes I worry about you. You need the trip to Africa more than Dmitri and I. In fact, you should visit India, take up meditation."

"Don't be silly! I'm perfectly happy with my life."

It appeared Ella was not as calm and composed as he'd thought. The brief flare of irritation revealed she was human, after all.

From his position beside the bed stand, Yevgeny switched his attention to the younger McLeod sister. Keira was biting her lip.

"You were going to ask Keira about names." Yevgeny spoke into the silence that had settled over the ward following Ella's curt response.

"Names?" Ella's poise slipped further. "Oh, yes." Yevgeny waited.

Keira twisted her head and glanced at him, a question in her eyes. "What names are you talking about?"

His brows jerked together. "The names you've been considering for the baby." His sister-in-law shouldn't need a prompt. The baby was so firmly in the forefront of his mind, how could it not be the same for her...and for Ella? What was wrong with these McLeod women?

"I hadn't chosen one yet."

"That's what I told him," Ella added quickly, protectively, her hand closing over her sister's where it rested on the edge of the bed. "Keira, you don't need to think about it if it upsets you...."

Relief flooded Keira's face as she turned away from him and said, "Ella, you're the best. I knew you would take care of everything."

Those words set his teeth on edge.

Shifting away from the sisters, Yevgeny crossed the room. Foreboding filled him.

Keira's confidence in her sister didn't reassure Yevgeny one bit. Because it was clear to him that Ella couldn't wait to get rid of the baby.

And that was the last thing he wanted.

Despite all the drama of the day, Ella surprised herself by managing to get several hours sleep that night.

Yet she still woke before the first fingers of daylight appeared through the crack in the curtains. For a long while she lay staring into space, thinking about what needed to happen. Finally, as dawn arrived, filling the ward with a gentle wash of December sun, she switched on the over-bed light and reached into the drawer of the bed stand for the legal pad she'd stowed there yesterday.

By the time the day nurse bustled in to remind her that the baby would be brought in from the nursery in fifteen minutes for the appointment with the pediatrician, Ella had already scribbled pages of notes. After a quick shower, she put on a dab of makeup and dressed in a pair of gray trousers and a white T-shirt. Then she settled into one of the pair of padded visitor chairs near the window to await the doctor's arrival.

The baby was wheeled in at the same time that the pediatrician scurried into the room, which—to Ella's great relief—meant that she wasn't left alone with the wide-awake infant. The doctor took charge and proceeded to do a thorough examination before pronouncing the baby healthy.

Tension that Ella hadn't even known existed seeped away with the doctor's words. The baby was healthy. For the first time she acknowledged how much she'd been dreading that something might be wrong. Of course, a well baby would benefit by having many more potential sets of adoptive parents wanting to love and cherish her.

After the pediatrician departed, the nurse took the baby back to the nursery, and Ella's breakfast arrived in time to stem the blossoming regret. Fruit, juice and oatmeal along with coffee much more aromatic than any hospital was reputed to produce.

Ella had just finished enjoying a second cup when Jo Wells entered her room. Ella had been pleased when she'd discovered that Jo had been assigned to processing the baby's adoption to Keira and Dmitri. Of course, that had all changed. Now she was even more relieved to have Jo's help.

Slight with short, dark hair, the social worker had a firm manner that concealed a heart of gold. Ella had worked with Jo a few times in the past. Once in a legal case where a couple wanted to adopt their teen daughter's baby, and more recently in a tough custody battle where the father had threatened to breach a custody order and kidnap his children to take them back to his home country.

"How are you doing?"

The understanding in Jo's kind eyes caused Ella's throat to tighten. She waved Jo to the other visitor seat, reached for the yellow legal pad on the bed stand and gave the social worker a wry smile. "As well as can be expected in the circumstances— This is not the outcome I'd planned."

Jo nodded with a degree of empathy that almost shredded the tight control Ella had been exercising since Keira had dropped her bombshell—was it only yesterday?

"I want the best for the baby, Jo."

Focusing on what the baby needed helped stem the tears that threatened to spill. Ella tore the top three pages off the pad and offered them to the social worker.

"I knew you'd ask. So I've already listed the qualities I'd like to see in the couple who adopts her. It would be wonderful if the family has an older daughter—perhaps two years older." That way the baby would have a bond like the one Ella shared with Keira, but the age difference would be smaller. Hopefully the sisters would grow up to be even closer than she and Keira were. "If possible, I'd like for her to be the younger sister—like Keira is. But above all, I'd like her to go to a family who will love her…care for her…give her everything that I can't."

Another nod. Yet instead of reading the long wish list that had taken Ella so much soul-searching in the dark hours this morning to compile, Jo pulled the second chair up. Propping the manila folder she'd brought with her against a bent knee, she spread the handwritten pages Ella had given her on top.

Then Jo looked up. "I spoke to Keira before coming here. She and Dmitri haven't had second thoughts."

Ella had known that. From the moment Keira had told her of their decision yesterday, she'd known Keira was not going to change her mind. But deep down she must have harbored a last hope because her breath escaped in a slow, audible hiss.

"Is there anyone else in the family who would consider adopting the baby?" Jo asked.

"My parents have just reached their seventies." Ella had been born to a mother already in her forties and Keira had followed five years later. "They've just moved into a retirement village. There's no chance that they're in a position to care for a newborn."

Even if they'd wanted to adopt the child, she wouldn't allow it. Her parents had already been past parenting when she and Keira had reached their teens. She was not letting this baby experience the kind of distant, disengaged upbringing they'd experienced.

"And we have no other close family," she tacked on.

"What about the biological father's family?"

An image of Yevgeny hovering over the bed last

night like some angel of vengeance flashed into Ella's mind. His pale, wolflike eyes filled with determination. His expression downright dangerous as she resisted what he wanted.

She dismissed the image immediately and said, "There's no one to my knowledge—his parents are dead." A pang of guilt seared her. Reluctantly she found herself correcting herself. "He does have an older brother. Yevgeny. But he's far from suitable."

Jo tilted her head to one side. "In what way is Yevgeny not suitable?"

"He's single—for one thing. The adoption laws don't allow single men to adopt female babies." Ella didn't mention Yevgeny's rash vow to marry to flout her plans.

"Except in exceptional circumstances…" Jo's voice trailed away as she bent her head and made a note on the cover of the manila file resting in her lap. "The court may consider his relationship to the baby sufficient."

"It's unlikely." Ella didn't want Jo even considering Yevgeny as a candidate—or learning that he intended to get married for the baby's sake.

But Jo wasn't ready to be deflected. "Hmm. We could certainly consider interviewing him."

Jo would discover that Yevgeny was determined to adopt the baby.

Ella's heart started to knock against her ribs. *No.* This wasn't what she wanted for the baby. Even if he did marry, Yevgeny would farm the baby out to a series of stunning Russian nannies and continue with his high-flying, jet-set lifestyle. Growing up with Yevgeny would be a far worse experience than the distracted neglect she and Keira had suffered.

"He's a playboy—he has a different woman every week."

That assessment was probably a little harsh, Ella conceded silently. He'd been linked to Nadiya for several months and before that he'd been single for a while—according to Keira. Although that hadn't stopped him from dating a string of high-profile women.

"And he's a workaholic," she added for good measure just in case Jo was still considering Yevgeny. Then she played her trump card. "He certainly won't provide the kind of stable home that I always intended for the child. I don't want the baby going to him."

"Being the legal mother, your wishes will take precedence." Jo tapped her pen against her knee. "This is still going to be an open adoption, right?"

An open adoption meant keeping in touch with the new adoptive parents, watching the baby grow up, being part of her life, yet not a parent.

Ella swallowed.

This was the hard part.

"Ella?" Concern darkened Jo's eyes as she failed to respond. "Research has shown open adoptions are far more beneficial because—"

"They give the child a sense of history and belonging, and help prevent the child having identity crises as a teen and in later life," Ella finished. She knew all the benefits. She'd had a long time to ponder over all the arguments. "We'd planned an open adoption with Keira and Dmitri. The baby would always know I was her tummy mummy—" now the affectionate term for a surrogate rang false in her ears "—her birth mother...even though Keira would be her real mother."

"So it will still be an open adoption?"

Ella nodded slowly. "It's in the baby's best interests."

But dear God, it was going to kill her.

Ella was relieved that Jo hadn't asked whether she would consider keeping the baby. She'd already emphatically told both Keira and Yevgeny she couldn't do it. A third denial would've been more than she could handle at this stage.

Jo's head was bent, eyes scanning the wish list Ella had given her.

Finally she looked up. "I have several sets of IPs—

intending parents—" Jo elaborated, "who might fit your requirements. I'll pull their profiles out and bring them back for you to look through."

"Thank you." Gratitude flooded Ella. "You have no idea how much of a help it is knowing you are here for support."

"It's my job." But Jo's warm eyes belied the words. "When will you be going home?"

"Probably tomorrow."

"And the baby?"

"The baby will go to a foster carer." Ella was determined not allow any opportunity for a maternal bond to form.

"I know you probably don't want to hear this, but you should reconsider your decision not to have counseling after you sign the final consent to give the baby up." Without looking at her, Jo shuffled the wish list into the manila file. Getting to her feet she pushed the visitor chair back against the wall before turning to face Ella. "I know you said previously that you didn't feel you'd need counseling because she was never intended to be your baby—that it was your gift to Keira and Dmitri. But given that circumstances have changed, I think it would be a serious mistake. You'll be experiencing a lot of emotions, which you never expected."

Ella resisted the urge to close her eyes and shut out

the world. Signing the consent could only be done on the twelfth day. She didn't want to even think about the approaching emotional maelstrom.

So she gave Jo a small smile. "I'll think about it," she conceded. "But I don't think it will be necessary. I'm tougher than I look."

Before Jo could reply, footsteps echoed outside the ward.

A moment later, Yevgeny appeared in the doorway. Ella's heart sank.

"This is Dmitri's brother, Yevgeny." She made the introduction reluctantly, and hoped that Jo would depart quickly.

To her dismay Jo and Yevgeny took their time sizing each other up. Only once they'd taken each other's measure, shaken hands and exchanged business cards, did Jo finally walk to the door. Ella let out the breath she'd been holding. Neither had even mentioned the baby's adoption.

Disaster averted.

For now.

"We'll talk again," the social worker said from her position in the doorway, giving Ella a loaded look over her shoulder. "I'll be back."

This morning Yevgeny was wearing a dark gray suit that fitted beautifully.

Towering over the chair she sat on, with the light behind him, Ella could see that his dark hair was still a touch damp—evidence of a recent shower, perhaps.

It was only as he tilted his head to look down at her that she noticed the stubble shadowing his jawline. A dazzling white shirt with the top button undone stood in stark contrast to his dark face.

Ella was suddenly desperately glad that she was not in bed.

Yesterday she'd felt at a terrible disadvantage as he'd towered over her while she'd been clad in a nightdress. She'd felt exposed...vulnerable. Even now, seated, his height was intimidating. But at least she could rectify that...

She rose to her feet. "The baby is in the nursery."

"I know—I have already been to visit her."

Annoyance flared. She had not been consulted. "They let you in?"

The staff would have to be told he was not welcome in the future—she wouldn't put it past him to try and take the baby. This was a man accustomed to getting his own way. But not this time.

Some indefinable emotion glimmered deep in the deceptively clear depths of his eyes. "Keira and Dmitri were with me—they vouched for me."

"Keira's here?"

Had her sister had second thoughts since Jo had spoken to her?

Yevgeny was shaking his head. "They've gone. Dmitri has quite a bit to finalize before I can release him to fly across the world."

All Ella could think of was that Keira hadn't even bothered to come past and say good morning. Hurt stabbed her. Then she set it aside. No doubt Keira was avoiding her because deep down her sister must be experiencing some guilt for the decision she and Dmitri had made.

Ella decided she wasn't going to let herself dwell on the turmoil that Keira's choice had created.

It was done.

Now there was the baby to think about....

But Yevgeny's response caused her to realize that she hadn't even asked her sister when they planned to leave for Africa. She'd been too busy trying to cope with the magnitude of the shock. Keira had said she and Dmitri had already booked the tickets but that's all she knew.

"Do you have any idea when they plan to leave?" It rankled to have to depend on Yevgeny for information but she needed to know.

"I believe they leave the day after tomorrow."

"That soon?"

Ella was still absorbing this new upset when he asked, "What will you be thinking about?"

"Pardon?" For a moment Ella thought Yevgeny had picked up on her earlier hurt at Keira's failure to come say good morning and was asking about her thoughts.

"You told the social worker you'd think about it." Yevgeny had moved up beside her, causing the space in the ward to shrink. "What will you be thinking about?"

Ella frowned as she realized he'd overheard the last part of her discussion with Jo. She had no intention of revealing that Jo thought she needed counseling. The good thing was at least he hadn't detected her hurt over Keira. "It's nothing important," she said dismissively. "It wasn't about the baby."

"Did you tell her I am going to adopt the baby?"

"But you're not." Inside, her stomach started to twist into a pretzel. Ella pursed her lips. "I told her you weren't suitable."

"You did not!"

"Yes, I did."

His gaze blitzed into her. "Because I'm single?"

Ella didn't glance away from his hard stare. "Among other things."

"But once I'm married that will change," he said softly and came another step closer. "You know that."

Ella blinked. And found herself inhaling the warm scent of freshly showered male. This close she could see the crisp whiteness of his ironed shirt.

What was he up to now?

"You should've seen her." His voice took on a husky, intimate tone. "She's so beautiful—"

Ella recoiled. "I don't care what your wife-to-be looks like!"

At her interruption, he looked puzzled, then he smiled. A smile filled with a burst of charm and humor that Ella hadn't wanted to recognize in Yevgeny Volkovoy. It made him all too human. And irresistibly appealing. This wouldn't do at all. She wanted—no, needed—to keep thinking of him as Keira's overbearing, bullying brother-in-law.

"No, not my wife-to-be. The baby." He chuckled. "She was awake…waving her hands and watching them. Smart *and* beautiful. You've seen her this morning."

It was a statement—rather than a question.

Ella squirmed, reluctant to admit that she'd barely glanced at the baby while she was in the ward during the pediatrician's consultation. Then she told herself she had no reason to feel guilty. Keira and Dmitri's actions were not her fault.

Rather than answering his question, she changed

the subject. "So you're going through with it? You're really going to get married?"

He nodded. "I want that baby."

God, the man was stubborn. Didn't he ever accept no for an answer? Time for him to learn he couldn't always get what he wanted in life. Sometimes someone else's needs came first.

This time, the baby's best interests were paramount. Not his.

Letting out the breath she'd been unconsciously holding since that first whiff of his male essence, Ella said, "Well, you need to know that you're sacrificing yourself for nothing. I'm not going to change my mind. And it's still my decision. As the legal mother, I get to choose the parents the baby will go to."

He went deadly still. "You will choose me—and my wife."

Was that a threat?

Ella carefully assessed his motionless body, the face with the high Slavic cheekbones, skin stretched taut across them. Yevgeny needed to know she wasn't going to let him bully her.

"Unlikely. This morning I gave Jo a list of the qualities I'm seeking in the prospective parents. Nothing you can offer meets the criteria. She's going to bring me portfolios of prospective parents to look at—and I'll choose a couple from there."

The tension in the air became electric. "When?"

"Shouldn't you be at work doing whatever it is that high-powered billionaires do?" Ella knew she was being deliberately provocative, but she'd never expected him to be this concerned about the baby.

"When?" he repeated, his face tight.

He wasn't going to relent, she realized. "As soon as I'm back home—tomorrow probably."

"And then what happens?"

"The couples have already been interviewed and screened. Police checks have been done. Once I choose a couple and the consent is signed, then the paperwork for the adoption can be filled in and submitted."

"The consent?"

"Yes." Ella explained further, "The legal mother can only sign the consent—that's the formal document where she agrees to give up the baby— on the twelfth day. And yesterday, the day the baby was born, counts as the first day."

From where she stood Ella could sense the intensity of his gaze. He wasn't smiling anymore. He was watching her, his head tipped slightly to one side, his brain working overtime. Yevgeny was busy hatching a fiendish plot. She was certain of it.

There was something curiously exhilarating about being the focus of all that raw, brilliant energy. He might come in a devastatingly well-groomed, freshly scented and well-built male package, but it was his mind that Ella found fascinating. That ability to concentrate with such single-minded intensity. The ability to conjure up solutions no one had come up with before.

She could kind of understand why women might be attracted to that....

"So you can change your mind anytime up until that twelfth day?" he asked.

Ella blinked—and wrenched herself away from her fancies. "In theory. But I wouldn't do it. It wouldn't be very fair to do that to a couple once I've told them they've been chosen."

Determination fired in his eyes. "This baby will be mine—I will do everything in my power to make sure that happens."

Despite the morning sunshine spilling through the windows of the ward, Ella shivered.

It was evening.

The sun was setting beyond the distinctive silhouette of the Auckland Bridge transforming the Waitemata Harbour to liquid gold. Turning his head away from the magnificent view, Yevgeny dropped down onto the king-size bed in Nadiya's hotel suite and gazed contemplatively across at the woman standing in front of the dresser, the woman he planned shortly to reduce to screaming satisfaction.

Yet instead of dwelling on the pleasures of seduction, his mind was already elsewhere.

It was the end of day two. He had only ten days left. Yevgeny knew he needed to act—and fast.

He had to get engaged—and he needed to convince Ella to change her mind about his suitability to be a father.

That was going to take some doing.

It was enough to make him grind his teeth with frustration. Yet he was a long way from conceding defeat. He'd never been the kind of man to back away from a challenge—and this was the most important challenge of his life.

Now or never.

Taking a deep breath, he gave Nadiya his most practiced smile and patted the bedcover beside him. "Come make yourself comfortable."

Nadiya glided across the room. Kicking off her high heels, she settled herself on the bed beside him. Long fingertips reached for the buttons of her silk shirtdress, and she gave him a pout.

"How do you feel about children?"

"Children?"

Nadiya's eyes widened, and her fingers stilled in the act of undressing. Her lips, still plump with gloss, parted. Yevgeny could identify with her shock. *He* was shocked. This was a discussion he had never before conducted with a woman. It was breaking new ground. But not only had he always desired Nadiya, he'd always liked her, too—even though, for the first time, he struggled to focus on their approaching lovemaking.

She hesitated, and then said, "I've always wanted children."

This was good.

Coming up on his elbow, he propped his hand under his head. "I am pleased to hear that."

From across the pale pink satin comforter, with her long legs folded beneath her, she watched him through those catlike eyes. "So you want children?"

What choice did he have? There was a child…and he couldn't walk away from her. But he wasn't ready to reveal more. So he gave Nadiya the same answer he'd given Ella. "The time has come."

She said, "I do have contractual obligations."

This wasn't what he needed to hear. Talk of contracts reminded him too much of…Ella.

He rolled away and lay back. She, too, was proving to be like the woman he tried never to think about.

Keeping his voice level, he said, "You don't have time for children."

"No, no. I'm not saying that!" Nadiya edged closer and placed her hand over his. "But I never expected you to offer—"

She broke off.

Sensing opportunity, he turned his head. "You never expected me to offer…what?"

"What *are* you offering, Yevgeny? You haven't actually said."

This was another thing he liked about Nadiya—she was direct. He chuckled softly, secure that he was about to get what he wanted. The sensation that shot through him was familiar; the dart of adrenaline that signified the successful conclusion of a deal. "I'm offering a diamond ring to the mother of my child."

"Marriage?"

He nodded. For one uncertain instant he considered telling her about the baby girl he planned to adopt… but before he could speak, Nadiya let out a breathy little gasp and started to bounce on the bed. "Yes! Yes! Yes!"

A wave of euphoria swept him. The first step of his plan had been accomplished. Ella McLeod would stand no chance.…

But why was he thinking about *her* when he should

be focused on Nadiya? Tightening his fingers around his fiancée's, he prompted, "And what about your contract?"

"We will work something out—I do want a baby."

Yevgeny studied her from under hooded eyelids. It might be a good idea to wait…to see how she reacted to the baby before he showed his hand entirely. The brief moment of uncertainty passed. Nadiya was beautiful, no doubt about that. Sexy, too. And beneath the model-perfect exterior she was likable. Everything a man could ever want. Everything he should be desiring.…

So why did he keep remembering a pair of outraged honey-gold eyes?

Four

Yevgeny returned to the hospital late the following afternoon—with his supermodel in tow. His face wore no expression as the pair entered the family waiting room where Ella had just met with Jo, and now she tried desperately to match his insouciance. All day, she'd found herself wondering when he would arrive.

Now he was here.

And he hadn't come alone.

Sitting on one of the two-seater love seats, her overnight bag already packed and ready to go, Ella couldn't help wishing that she'd taken the time to blow-dry her hair straight after breakfast instead of wasting time staring out the hospital-ward window for thirty soul-searching minutes. Now, at the end of the day, her hair hung like rats' tails around her face while Nadiya looked absolutely fabulous. Not that Ella should care...but unaccountably she did.

Maybe she couldn't look as if she'd stepped out the pages of *Vogue,* but she wanted to look capable and together—like someone out of a feature on successful women in *Cosmo.*

Brisk. Businesslike. A woman who had achieved every career goal she'd ever set for herself; not the quivering mass of Jell-O–like uncertainty that she was right now.

Nadiya was glancing around the family room with interest—taking in the large black-and-white photos of mothers cradling babies that decorated the walls. Ella wondered if she'd ever seen inside a maternity unit before. Given the model's whippet-slim figure, pregnancy was not something Ella could imagine the supermodel contemplating with glee.

"Where's the baby?"

Ella managed not to roll her eyes skyward. Of course the baby would be the first thing that Yevgeny asked about.

"Her diaper is being changed."

"The birth went well?" asked Nadiya.

Ella could've hugged the woman for unwittingly preventing Yevgeny from venting the criticism that hovered unspoken on his lips. Clearly he thought *she* should be attending to the baby.

"Yes, very well." She gave the supermodel a small smile. "I've already been discharged."

"That's good. How much does she weigh?"

Ella told her.

"Your sister must be thrilled—she's changing her now?"

Did Nadiya not know that Keira had pulled out of the adoption? Ella's questioning gaze slid to Yevgeny. Perhaps the two weren't as close as she'd assumed...perhaps Nadiya was not the bride he intended to sucker into marriage.

"I—"

"I brought Nadiya to meet the baby," he cut in before Ella could respond. "She has agreed to marry me." He lifted Nadiya's hand to flash a gigantic diamond, and smirked at Ella.

"No!" She realized she'd said it out loud as Nadiya's face reflected shock. "I mean...what a surprise."

The other woman's eyes had narrowed and she was studying Ella in a way that made her feel decidedly uncomfortable. Nadiya's gaze flashed back and forth between Ella and Yevgeny. Her discomfort increased. The conclusion the other woman was drawing about Ella's hasty objection was wrong.

She hastened to correct her. "You don't understand—"

"Let's go visit the baby." Nadiya smiled up at Yevgeny as her fingers walked up his arm then spread out and rested against his suit-clad biceps in an unmistakably possessive gesture. The diamond sparkled. The model turned her head, and her gaze glittered *mine* at Ella.

Nadiya was welcome to the man!

As the pair exited the ward, Ella glared at Yevgeny's retreating back. He was the most devious, cold-bloodedly scheming man she'd ever come across—and she'd seen enough. He'd gone out to find the first woman to marry him—and proposed—without bothering to explain *why* he wanted to marry her.

He was using the young woman.

Deep down, Ella knew she was being unfair. Nadiya might be young but she was far from naive. And what man wouldn't want to marry Nadiya?

But at the back of her mind, worry raged for the baby. Given a choice, a fashion model was hardly the kind of mother she would've picked out. Together, as a couple, Yevgeny and Nadiya were so far removed from her notion of ideal parents. This was a train crash waiting to happen…and the baby would be the biggest victim.

Even as anxiety noodled her stomach into a tangle

of nerves, one of the caregivers bustled in. "I've changed the baby. Mr. Volkovoy and his friend are with her in the nursery. The baby is looking well. She'll be fine to leave." She stopped beside Ella and said in a tone of inquiry, "Jo said the adoption is still some time away from being finalized."

Not if Yevgeny had his way....

But Ella was far from convinced that the Russian billionaire and his supermodel fiancée were the kind of parents the baby deserved. The last thing she wanted was to read about the baby in the tabloids and gossip magazines as so often happened with celebrities who seemed to care little for their offspring.

She might not be in a position to keep the baby. But she could damn well make sure it got the best start in life—and that meant the best parents possible.

And she'd told Jo that in as many words.

The five profiles she'd gone through with Jo earlier before rejecting them all had confirmed Jo's statement that there were many parents anxiously waiting to adopt. But Ella had a sinking feeling that Yevgeny's insistence to adopt might still prove a hindrance.

"The baby will stay with a foster family until I choose the final adoptive parents," Ella answered at last.

"That will be one very happy set of parents," the caregiver said, drawing the curtains farther back to let more light into the room.

There was nothing more to say.

Ella knew it was time to pick up the overnight bag she'd packed hours ago and for her to leave the place where she'd given birth—and leave the baby behind.

But before Ella got a chance to gather up her overnight bag and make her escape, Yevgeny and Nadiya returned—with the baby. Wheeling the cot into the middle of the room, Yevgeny bent forward to lift her out.

Ella closed her eyes. Every muscle tensed. *Don't give her to me. Don't give her to me.* The frantic refrain echoed through her head. She hadn't wanted to see the baby before she left. Ella had hoped that the next time she saw her, the baby would be securely in her new parents' home.

A gurgling sound broke into her desperation.

"She's grinning!"

Ella opened her eyes. Yevgeny was holding the baby up, one big hand cradling the back of her neck. Face-to-face with the baby, his strong masculine profile provided a sharp contrast to the baby's swaddled softness. She looked tiny against this big hulk. Ella tensed further. What if he dropped her?

"Careful!"

He didn't even look at her; all his attention was focused on the baby.

"Look, she's laughing."

Nadiya leaned in toward the two of them, resting long slim fingers on Yevgeny's arm, her silky sable hair spilling over his shoulder. "Babies that young don't laugh. She's yawning."

A jab pierced Ella's heart at the sight of the three dark heads so close together. To her horror she felt her throat tighten. She swallowed. The tightness swelled more.

She couldn't have said anything even if she hadn't felt so awful.

"No, that's not a yawn—it's laughter," the billionaire insisted.

Nadiya moved even closer, and Ella was sure that Yevgeny and the baby would be asphyxiated by Nox Parfum fumes.

"This is something I know a lot about," Nadiya said. "I've handled many babies… I've got four sisters and about a dozen nieces and nephews." Nadiya took the baby from him with an easy competence that Ella found herself envying.

Maybe Yevgeny hadn't made such a mistake in picking the supermodel to marry. Clearly Nadiya knew something about babies—despite her glamorous exterior.

Loneliness swamped Ella, dismaying her. To ward it off, she said, "You're happy to adopt her?"

Startled eyes met hers. "Adopt her?"

Yevgeny moved. All too soon he stood between Ella and his bewildered fiancée like some oversize sentinel. He shot Ella a fulminating look.

"Nadiya and I have yet to discuss the specifics."

No…it wasn't possible, he couldn't have been that…arrogant…that dumb. Could he?

Over the head of the oblivious baby, the super-model's attention shifted to her fiancé. "The specifics of what?"

Yes, he'd been that dumb.

He hadn't told Nadiya.

Now he looked hunted. Then he smiled at his fiancée—a slow, deliberate smile that oozed intimacy. "We will talk later. In private."

Ella watched as he gave the supermodel a slow once-over that was clearly intended to turn her legs to water. She knew she should've experienced distaste at the obvious sexual manipulation he was using on the young woman. Instead, to her utter dismay, her own stomach started to churn at the blatant sensuality in that hard-boned face. What would it feel like to be the object of this man's desire?

To have him gaze at *her* with such unwavering intensity?

Heat, wanton—no, *unwanted*—blazed through her.

To rid herself of the emotional storm she didn't want, Ella said with a coolness she was far from feeling, "Yevgeny intends to adopt the baby."

Nadiya stared down at the wrapped infant in her arms. "This baby?" She lifted her head and turned her attention to her fiancé. "But why?"

"He didn't explain it to you—that I told him he needed a wife?"

Ella couldn't stem the words.

Pity for the younger woman filled her. Yevgeny hadn't taken Nadiya's wishes into account. He'd simply assumed she would fall in with what he wanted. Once again he was putting what he wanted first, not thinking of anyone else. What arrogance! The dislike Ella already felt toward him escalated, not helped by that surge of awareness that he had unwittingly aroused.

But to Ella's surprise, Nadiya was glaring at him. "You asked me if I wanted children..." As her voice trailed away, the frown marring her forehead deepened. "You weren't talking about the future, you were talking about now. About this baby."

"Nadiya—"

But Nadiya held up a hand, interrupting whatever he'd been about to say. A couple of quick steps brought her to Ella's side and she deposited the baby into Ella's lap. The baby started to cry—a gruff, growly sound that caused Ella to freeze. She stared down at the crumpled, red face and panic pierced her.

What the hell was she supposed to do now?

From a distance she could hear Nadiya angrily saying something to Yevgeny, but Ella was in no state to listen. She stroked the baby with a tentative hand. The cries continued. Awkwardly she patted the baby's back…then rocked her a little. There was a pause. The tightly pressed eyelids opened. The baby's eyes were a dark shade of midnight. Ella stared, transfixed.

"You need to support her neck."

The voice came from far off. The words were repeated and a hand with a flashing diamond appeared in Ella's peripheral vision. It cupped her own.

"There. Like that," said Nadiya.

Ella looked up. "Thank you."

But Nadiya had already spun to confront Yevgeny. Ella couldn't look away as Nadiya hissed, "Why this child?" Her hands were on her hips. She shot a quick look over her shoulder at Ella, then moved her attention back to the Russian. "Is it your child?"

"Nadiya—"

"Answer me!"

Holding the now quiet infant, Ella wanted to cheer.

But before she could make any sound, Nadiya's gaze arced to her "...and yours?"

That was taking it too far. It was one thing to needle Yevgeny, but Ella didn't want anyone thinking she'd slept with this bully.

"No!" said Ella. "This is not his child—it's Dmitri's child!"

Confusion misted Nadiya's eyes. "So where is Dmitri?" Her attention swung to Yevgeny. "And why are you talking about adopting your brother's child?"

He really hadn't told Nadiya anything at all.

"Because my brother and his wife have decided they no longer want a baby. She's of my blood. How can I let her go to strangers?"

There lay the key to his behavior—he was prepared to sacrifice his own freedom for the baby's sake to prevent a person he believed belonged to his family from going to strangers.

Nadiya's gaze moved back to Ella. "And you are the mother, right? Not your sister?"

Why did Nadiya have to put it like that? Ella rocked the baby a little more. "I'm *not* the planned mother—Keira is. Or was supposed to be," she amended. "I'm only a surrogate."

She couldn't help feeling the stab of a traitor's guilt.

"You only carried the baby?"

Ella wriggled uncomfortably before conceding, "The eggs are mine, too."

"So you are the mother." Nadiya cut to the heart of it.

Ella shifted again. The baby mewed. A quick glance revealed that the baby's face had puckered up. Oh, no, she was about to cry again. Ella rocked harder; the puckers relaxed a little. She risked raising her head. "Biologically, yes. Legally, yes. Morally, no."

Over the baby's head, Nadiya gave her a long, searching look. Then she turned to Yevgeny. "You should have told me. You knew I believed you were asking me to have *my* baby."

"It makes a difference?" Yevgeny's gaze was hooded.

"Yes. My career is demanding right now, but I would take time off for my baby. My baby—and yours."

"But not for this baby?"

Nadiya looked tormented.

"That's not fair!" Unable to keep quiet at his

hectoring, Ella rose to the younger woman's defense. In her arms the soft body of the baby stiffened. Ella made a mental note to keep her voice level.

"You've already caused enough trouble. You stay out of this," he snarled.

"But she's right. You're not being fair—and I'm not going to do this." Nadiya was tugging the great glittering ring off her finger.

"Wait—"

"No, this isn't going to work. I thought you loved me…that you were talking about us having a baby together. But you were using me!" Fury sparkled in her green eyes. She thrust the ring at him, her fingers shaking. "Take it."

The baby carefully cradled on her lap, Ella drew back into the chair and tried to make herself invisible. Some things deserved privacy. And it was uncomfortable to watch Nadiya's pain as moisture glimmered in her eyes. There was hurt…and anger… and something else that made Ella wince.

It startled her to realize that the model had loved the ruthless Russian. The revelation made Ella furious. Poor, hoodwinked Nadiya.

A woman would have to be incredibly shortsighted to fall in love with him. Yet Nadiya clearly had. Being beautiful and successful hadn't saved her from being devastated by his effortless manipulation.

The tableau playing itself out in front of her brought back old hurts…humiliations…that Ella had hoped were long forgotten.…

She never intended to feel like that about any man ever again.

Particularly not a man like Yevgeny Volkovoy.

Nadiya tossed back her head, and her hair rippled like black silk in the light. "No one uses me."

Yevgeny didn't respond. He simply stood there staring down at the woman he'd so recently announced was his fiancée.

"Pah…you're not even prepared to deny it. I feel sorry for you, Yevgeny. You don't recognize the importance of love. But one day you're going to fall in love with someone—real love—and she's going to rip your heart out, just like you've ripped mine out." Wiping the tears away, the supermodel straightened to her glamorous full height. "You're not worth crying over."

"You did that deliberately!" Yevgeny blew out a pent-up breath as the rapid tap-tap of Nadiya's skyscraper heels receded down the corridor.

Ella didn't even flinch at his accusation. "What do you mean?"

Her voice was softer than he expected.

It gave him a strange feeling to see her holding the

baby that he already adored. So he looked away from the infant and pinned the most irritating woman he'd ever met under his gaze. "You caused that scene you just witnessed."

"*I* caused it?" Her eyes widened. "I simply told the poor woman the truth. Don't blame me. You should've explained things to her."

Perhaps Ella had a point.

But he'd wanted to assess Nadiya's reaction to the baby first—and it had been more than he'd hoped for. He and Nadiya had never talked much about family…or children. They hadn't shared that kind of relationship. Yet when Nadiya had taken the baby into her arms like a woman created for motherhood, and revealed she was used to her sister's children, Yevgeny had been overcome by relief. He couldn't have gotten a better outcome if he'd planned it for a month. And he'd thought the baby would be safe….

Then Ella had interfered.

He stared blankly at the woman he despised as she moved the baby to and fro in small motions.

Nadiya had made it clear she wasn't prepared to raise someone else's child. In seconds his plan had started to unravel and he could do nothing but watch impotently. It was all Ella's fault. Yet she didn't even want the baby. He could understand Nadiya's stance. It was more acceptable than the distinct lack of warmth that Ella exhibited toward a child she'd carried for nine months. That coldness, that lack of feeling, he would never grasp.

And Ella already had the next step planned—to identify a couple to adopt the child.

Which raised another thought. He'd seen Jo Wells waiting at the elevator when he and Nadiya had arrived. Had the social worker been to see Ella to discuss prospective parents?

Didn't Ella realize it was a waste of time choosing other parents? He was going to adopt the baby. What Ella didn't appear to get was that he was a man of immense financial reserves and infinite patience. Those attributes had made him into the mega-wealthy man he was today. He studied the fake Madonna-child tableau in front of him through narrowed eyes.

From her hesitation, it was clear that Ella had had little to do with babies. She knew as little about them as he did. But he was willing to learn—she wasn't. He wanted this baby…and he wasn't about to let her win this round.

The sooner she got that into her stubborn head, the better.

"Well, I no longer have the prospective wife you considered I need. But I still intend to adopt the baby." He was proud of the lack of emotion in his voice.

Ella's chin came up in a gesture he was starting to recognize. Instantly his muscles tensed.

"I've been looking at portfolios of couples who've already been screened. You have not been interviewed or checked yet."

That answered his unasked question. Jo *had* been here to discuss the baby's future parents. And it was equally obvious that his own proposal had not been on the agenda—because of Ella's prejudice against him.

"Then I'll have to remedy that," he said quietly. "This baby carries the blood of generations of Volkovoys in her veins—she is not leaving my family."

"Not even if it would be better for her?"

"You don't know that." He glanced down at the baby. Her mouth was moving up and down, tempting him to smile. But now was not a time to smile. "You could be letting the baby in for a life of hell."

"That's unlikely. The couples have been assessed and police checks carried out—"

"Who really knows what happens in the privacy of a couple's home? And do you really want to take that risk?"

That silenced Ella.

As color drained from her face, leaving it a pasty shade of white, Yevgeny realized he'd overdone it. Of course, he didn't even believe his own alarmist statement—he and Dmitri might have been better off adopted by a loving couple than ordered by a bamboozled judge to stay with his mother after his parents' divorce. But if his scaremongering changed Ella's mind, then it would be worth it.

The end justified the means; he'd always lived his life by that creed.

Yet unexpectedly, shame lingered within him as unhappiness and worry clouded her eyes. Her fingers had clenched, whitening her knuckles against the Disney print of the baby's swaddling wrap. He glanced away—and caught sight of Ella's overnight bag.

After a beat, he said, "Your bags are packed. You're leaving."

Ella nodded.

"The baby will be going with you."

He told himself she wouldn't walk away now that she'd held...engaged with...the baby. He waited for her affirmation of what he hoped to hear.

She shook her head. "No."

Ella intended to go through with her vow not to keep the baby. She would leave her daughter behind. What kind of woman would do that? Yevgeny still found it hard to believe she could be so callous. "You will leave the baby here?"

"The baby will go to a specially trained foster mother who will look after her until I pick the right family out for her. Jo and I discussed the foster mother earlier—she knows the baby is coming."

Two thoughts filled his head. *She* was made of ice, and how could she not understand that *he* was the right family!

Anger rose like a tidal wave.

Yevgeny reached for his wallet to retrieve the business card Jo Wells had given him the day before. His hands trembled at the emotion swamping him. "That will not happen. I am taking the baby home with me. I will call your social worker and tell her so."

"No!" yelled Ella from behind him. "If you take her, I'll have you arrested for kidnapping."

The baby started to cry.

Yevgeny stopped in his tracks at the sound and whipped around to face them. Ella was frantically rocking the baby—even uttering hoarse hushing sounds.

When the baby quieted, she met his gaze and said in a more even tone, "You need to think about the baby. It's not fair on her to form an attachment with you if she's going to be given to another family."

Angered and frustrated, he snapped, "If you would stop being so goddamned stubborn, you would know that she should stay with me—be my daughter."

"And how will that work?" A note he'd never heard from Ella before filled her voice. "You're never home. You work like a demon—don't deny it. Keira's told me all about how Dmitri's always exhausted."

He bit back the surge of irritation at his sister-in-law. "I'll rearrange my schedule."

"You really believe that?" Ella gazed at him from pitying eyes. "You're a type-A, high-achieving success junkie... You need your daily fix. Staying home with a baby will drive you crazy. You wouldn't last more than two days."

"What makes you think that?"

"Because I know." Her shoulders drooped as she blew out a breath, yet she didn't lower the baby; she continued to rock the bundle back and forth. She gave him a sad smile. "I am exactly the same—and people like us are not made to have children. Babies should be placed in families where they will have a better chance of being loved and living fruitful lives. Taking the baby would be a selfish thing to do. Why not be selfless and allow her the chance to be happy?"

The woman didn't know what she was talking

about. He and she were nothing alike. Yevgeny refused to listen to what she was saying.

Yet instead of challenging her claim, he countered, "And you think you're any less selfish?"

"What do you mean?"

"Christmas is coming." He gestured to the small tree standing in the corner of the waiting room. "And you're going to send the baby you gave birth to away to a foster home? Her first Christmas will be spent as an orphan. Alone. I will not allow it. I am calling Jo Wells now—I don't care how she arranges it, but that baby in your arms is going home with me. No baby should be alone at Christmas."

Five

Bringing the baby home was the most ill-considered thing she'd ever done, Ella decided ruefully the following morning.

She'd given up trying to get the baby to sleep an hour ago—after a night spent mixing formula and warming bottles and not a wink of sleep. A glance at the large white clock on the ivory-patterned wallpaper revealed it was already seven-thirty Monday morning. Normally she'd be in the office already, her emails read and answered. She'd be about to fetch the single cup of coffee she'd allowed herself each day during her pregnancy. Made from a fragrant, specially ground blend she favored, it was a must to kick-start her day.

This morning she hadn't even fired up her laptop…
much less thought about coffee.

Ella was exhausted.

But it was worth it.…

She'd refused to allow Yevgeny to all but kidnap
the baby and take it away with him. Once that
happened he would never let the baby go. She knew
that. The only way to stop that from happening
had been to take the baby home herself…and the
sacrifice was probably going to kill her.

At the very least, it was going to break what was
left of her heart.

She gazed wearily at the tiny girl-monster lying
on the plump couch beside her.

"Don't you think it's time for a nap?"

The baby stared back at her with round, wide-
awake eyes.

Ella sighed.

She had no idea what she was doing but the few
tips from a willing nurse that she'd scribbled down
on the legal pad before leaving the maternity unit
had been a godsend. At least the baby wouldn't
starve—she'd just finished a bottle. Yet it had only
reinforced how much Ella didn't know. After all, she
hadn't attended parenting classes or read any books
on child rearing during the pregnancy because that
had been Keira's department. She'd only read the

manuals about the dos and don'ts for the period the baby was growing in her stomach, none of which were of any help now.

Thank heavens she'd called an agency to engage a nanny before leaving the hospital yesterday. The agency hadn't been able to send someone at once, and Ella had wished she hadn't been so hasty in telling Yevgeny that she was taking the baby home, but pride hadn't let her back down.

How much trouble could a baby be?

She closed her eyes, thinking about the night past…trouble didn't even begin to describe the experience!

And after today there were still eight days to go before she could sign the adoption consent.

Ella didn't even want to contemplate it.

Opening her eyes, she gazed down at the baby, who was now wiggling her legs. Ella knew her biggest challenge was going to be maintaining a healthy distance from this child. What she didn't need was to form an attachment to a baby she had no intention of keeping. She'd hoped that the baby would spend most of the time asleep—after all, that was what had happened at the maternity unit.

But it certainly hadn't played out like that last night.…

Since they'd gotten home to Ella's cozy town

house, most of the baby's waking time had been spent in her arms. It seemed to have forgotten what sleep was. Ella had walked her up and down for what seemed like the whole night...to no avail.

Her cell phone beeped.

Ella reached for it and squinted at the hi-tech screen.

The messages had started early this morning— from colleagues and clients who had no idea of the baby's arrival on Friday evening, and thought this would be a normal work Monday. Ella knew she faced a flood of calls and emails...and that she ought to divert them to Peggy, her assistant...but right now she was too tired to move—or to think of anything.

Except sleep...

The baby chose that moment to burp.

As tired as she was, it was impossible not to smile. Ella forced her face straight. This was not the way to maintain a healthy distance. She shifted her attention back to the cell phone. Another message beeped through.

Then it rang.

It was the childcare agency she'd contacted yesterday to let her know the nanny had been dispatched.

Ella sighed with relief as she killed the call.

Wrinkling her nose at the child, she said, "Sleep is on its way."

She'd have to summon the energy to call the office, check that Peggy had canceled all her meetings for the day, and then she could crawl into bed. It was the stuff fantasies were made of....

The nanny turned out to be a short, energetic woman named Deb Benson. Within half an hour she'd restored order, unexpectedly leaving Ella feeling inadequate. She was used to making decisions, doing deals, dispensing advice, but as far as babies were concerned, she was a rookie. It was hard to accept how inept she was. Explaining the situation to Deb had also proved to be difficult—so, too, the fact that the baby didn't yet have a name. Yet Deb hadn't even blinked.

It made Ella wonder what it would take to faze her.

A lot more than a baby created for a couple who'd decided to give her up...and a surrogate mother who avoided cuddling her.

But it was for her own protection, Ella reminded herself as she made her way to the sleek white-and-silver home office where she spent much of her out-of-office time. Yet once barricaded in the familiar space, Ella struggled to concentrate. It wasn't the fact that she felt different—heck, it would've been impossible not to! Her stomach felt soft—no more gym-hard abs. Her breasts were swollen, tight and aching.

Having the baby had changed her body—and now, little as Ella wanted to admit it, the infant was changing her life.

Her silver laptop sat on the smooth, white desk. Ella flipped it open. She forced herself to call Peggy.

When she put the phone down she found that her ears were straining to hear what Deb was doing. She stared blindly at the screen in front of her. Against her will she found herself using Google to search "baby names" and faced with pages of websites. Most popular girls' names of the seventies…eighties… nineties…noughties…and beyond.

There were websites for flower names, for foreign names. Her mind boggled.

Lily. Rose. Petunia.

With a click of the mouse the next webpage opened.

Manon. Jeanne.

Another click.

Eleni. Roshni.

Ella clicked back to the first website with the botanical girls' names.

Or Holly.

The sound of the doorbell was an unwelcome interruption. Scant seconds later the door to her office burst open, and an even more unwelcome male presence filled the doorway.

"You've hired a nanny!"

Determined not to give Yevgeny more advantage than surprise had already afforded him, Ella shut the computer lid and rose to her feet. He dwarfed her. She swore silently. Next time she would wear heels.

"Of course I have." She met his outraged gaze as calmly as she was able. "I have a job to get back to."

"You're due maternity leave."

Ella shook her head. "I work for myself, so any leave I take is scheduled long in advance. This time I only allowed myself a few days off." And that had been next week. When the baby was supposed to arrive—not long before Christmas. "Anyway, I wasn't keeping the baby, remember? So I certainly didn't need maternity leave." And now, since Keira's bombshell, Ella knew she definitely didn't want to be sitting around with time to think.

His eyes glittered with disbelief. "And none of that has changed since bringing the baby home?"

She struggled with another wave of weariness and searched for words to explain her feelings to the man watching her as though she were some two-headed alien.

"How can it? I have to work." She stared back at him. *Attack was the best form of defense.* "You employ women—some of them might even be executives." Although she doubted it. Men like Yevgeny Volkovoy didn't take women seriously enough to give them significant responsibility. One only had to look at the women he dated— models, socialites—to see that. Although she had to admit that Nadiya had shown more spunk than Ella would've expected from one of his conquests— certainly more than Yevgeny wanted. "I can only imagine what you'd say about a woman who planned to be back at work, then decided to take several months off instead."

He blinked, and Ella saw the truth of her argument register.

He shrugged.

"Maybe." Then he added, "But I would've understood. Eventually." Putting his hands on his hips, he tilted his head to one side. "And that argument doesn't apply here—you are your own boss."

"Which means I can't just disappear from the office—I need to carefully plan the times away and arrange for someone to cover for me." And most important, she wanted to avoid becoming too attached to the child. "I *want* to go back to work."

"So when do you plan to do that?"

"As soon as I can." Ella didn't say "tomorrow," which was what she fully intended—so long as her body obliged and the fatigue that was starting to make her feel dizzy wasn't too much of a factor.

"And dump the child you haven't even given a name on the nanny?"

Ella stifled a yawn. "Holly will be perfectly happy."

"Holly? *Holly?*" He reared back. "You've named the baby?"

"Obviously."

He looked surprised. "Just now? To prove me wrong?"

"Not to prove you wrong! I picked her name earlier." She wasn't admitting to those minutes of scouring websites—after all, she couldn't even fathom what had driven her to do a Google search for baby names. It was all too uncomfortable to absorb. And why did he think she'd done it merely to prove him wrong? Let him think it had been an arbitrary name plucked out of the air. "You shouldn't assume an importance you don't have in my life."

But instead of causing Yevgeny to puff up with annoyance as she'd intended, her comment made him laugh.

"Bravo," he said.

Ella stared. Tiredness must be befuddling her. Because with his white teeth flashing and laugh lines—which she'd never noticed before—crinkling around his eyes, he caused her breath to hook in her throat. In the wickedly sparkling eyes, Ella got a glimpse of his appeal. This must be the reason women hung around him like bees around a honeypot.

The man looked devastating.

And all because she'd tried to put him in his place!

She couldn't help smiling back.

But his next words wiped the smile off her face.

"I came expecting to find you ready to beg me to take her away." His light eyes grew cloudy. "I should've known you'd hire a nanny."

He'd expected her to fail at the first hurdle.

That stung!

Because even though she'd hired a nanny to keep the baby at a distance, deep in her heart she knew he was right. She *had* failed. She was dangerously ignorant about babies, and it didn't help that her ignorance came because she'd never intended to have children of her own. It only served to underscore her secret, deeply held conviction that she would make a terrible parent.

Mostly his criticism stung because the truth of it was Ella wasn't accustomed to failure. Whatever task she undertook she saw through to the bitter end.

And arranging for the baby's adoption would be

no different—once she'd had a good-night's sleep and gotten herself back to normal.

But Yevgeny only saw a woman he didn't particularly like, so he wrote her off as useless— like he'd written most of her sex off. He was definitely archaic… She'd dearly love to see him taught a lesson. Tempting as it was to daydream that she might be the woman to do that, Ella knew it wouldn't—couldn't—be her. Some other woman would have to have the pleasure of taking him down a peg or two…one day. How she'd love to see the arrogant Yevgeny grovel.

"Didn't you come to see Holly?" she asked, too exhausted to get drawn into another of their fiery exchanges.

"Thanks to the nanny, she's probably been fed at least."

Annoyance surfaced, exacerbated by the mind-numbing weariness. Did he believe she would neglect the baby? Just because she didn't want a child didn't mean that she'd ever see it harmed. No, not *it…her*. Holly was a little girl. Ella sighed inwardly. It was hard enough to keep her distance to stop an attachment forming; she didn't need his cruel barbs. "I looked after her all night. The nanny only just arrived."

"Then I'd better go check on her."

Ella ground her teeth, and turned her head to stare blindly at her computer screen. Unable to help herself she blurted out, "None of the intending parents' profiles Jo Wells left at the hospital fit what I'm looking for."

It got so quiet, she thought Yevgeny must've already gone, that he hadn't heard her.

That might be for the best.

She turned her head, glanced over her shoulder.

Yevgeny stood as unmoving as a marble statue on the office's threshold, his pale eyes hungry and intent.

Waiting.

This was what he'd wanted to know, wasn't it? But Ella refused to hold out false hope. "Jo has already brought another batch of portfolios for me to look at. There should be at least one set of suitable parents there."

"You're choosing them tonight?"

She shook her head, flinching inwardly at the thought of what lay ahead. Glimpses into the lives of strangers desperate for a baby. And not just any baby—the baby she had helped create.

More hopeful faces would smile out of the pages at her—with carefully picked words detailing their dreams. Each set of parents hoping they would be the chosen ones. And if she liked more than one set, it would only get harder. After meeting the couples, she'd have to choose one couple over the other. Right now she couldn't face the mountain that lay ahead.

"I'll do it tomorrow." She turned away from the intensity that radiated from him, back to her laptop.

A moment later his footsteps receded. After the door closed softly behind him, Ella's shoulders sagged. She could barely concentrate on the letters on the screen in front of her. Giving in, she rose and went to sit on the love seat beneath the window, her computer perched on her stomach. Much more comfortable.

For the next few minutes, she'd see what appointments she could reschedule…then…then, she'd go see what Yevgeny was doing. See if she could hurry him along. Once Yevgeny had departed, she'd be able to relax. She'd go lie down in her bedroom.

And welcome the sleep her body craved.

Yevgeny pushed the door to Ella's office open with the flat palm of his hand and reentered the room. One glance caused him to pause.

The icicle had fallen asleep.

He crossed the room with silent steps, his footfalls muffled by the pile of the pale gray carpet until he stood beside the sofa.

Yet, instead of an icicle's cold clinical perfection, Ella's skin held a very feminine rosy flush. Her hair feathered across her forehead, the sharp-angled bob nowhere in evidence.

She looked younger. Prettier. *Softer.*

Yevgeny shrugged the illusion away.

Her laptop, angled across her midriff, was in danger of toppling off. She'd been working. Of course she had.

What had he expected?

That she'd been mothering? He suppressed a snort of disgust. The baby was where he'd just left her— in the arms of the nanny. His mouth compressing, he lifted the computer gently off Ella's stomach and set it down on her desk. Turning back, he took in the uncomfortable way she was draped over the small couch. Her feet, one hooked over the other, dangled over the edge and her body was skewed so that her bottom cheek was pressed against the white leather cushions. It definitely didn't look comfortable.

Bending over, he lifted her feet and laid them straight along the couch. Instantly they slid back over the edge. He stilled, fearing she might waken. But she didn't stir.

The way her body was twisted suggested she was going to wake with a God-Almighty crick in her neck for sure. Yevgeny didn't know why it was bothering him, but he couldn't leave her like this. When he'd first arrived, she'd looked tired with gray shadows rimming her expressive eyes. Leaving aside her lack of motherly instincts, Ella had been through a lot in the past few days. She'd given birth to the baby that her sister had given up. She'd had to cope with deciding the baby's future.

She must be worn out.

The first flicker of unwilling sympathy for her stirred within him.

He might not agree with the decisions she was planning, but he could appreciate how stressful it must be. He knelt and scooped her up against his chest. She made a tiny mewing sound, and her lashes fluttered. Then she burrowed in against his shoulder.

She smelt of a soft, old-fashioned scent.

Lilacs...

Yevgeny bit back a curse.

Straightening to his full six-foot, three-inch height, he strode out of the glossy white-and-gray office. At the end of the carpeted corridor a door stood ajar. With one foot, he knocked it wide to reveal what was clearly the main bedroom in the town house.

What a difference.

While white once again dominated, it wasn't the glossy white of leather and lacquer that he'd seen in the rest of the house. No reflective glass and silver mirrors in here. This was…

Holding her against him, he let his eyes travel around.

A bed decked out with snowy-white linen was the centerpiece of this pretty, feminine room. In his peripheral vision Yevgeny caught sight of a French-style dressing table with a collection of antique, glass perfume bottles and a set of silver-backed hairbrushes. His gaze stopped on two pairs of ballet shoes suspended by faded pink satin ribbons from an ornately carved brass hook. He started to smile. On the opposite wall hung a large acrylic painting of a dancer in a style reminiscent of Degas.

It was a bedroom filled with nostalgia and romance.

Not quite what he would've expected, given the brisk business exterior Ella McLeod presented to the world.

He entered the bedroom.

Instantly he was enveloped in a mist of that flowery, feminine scent—the scent he was fast coming to associate with the essence of Ella. Gently he laid her down on the pristine white linen of the bed, then stepped back. He could hear her breathing. Deep and even through slightly parted pale pink lips. Pale pink lips that held him enthralled.

Just one kiss…and she could waken.

The idea was ridiculous, but it persisted. Sense warred with temptation. Until, at last, he succumbed to the tantalizing temptation and bent forward. He placed the softest of kisses on her lips then straightened, his color high, feeling unaccountably foolish.

Ella didn't stir.

He'd gotten the legend wrong—she was not Sleeping Beauty—and instead of waking, the Ice Queen slept on.

It was already Tuesday. Keira and Dmitri had departed for Africa—without changing their minds about the baby. It had taken all Ella's willpower not to scream at her sister that she was making the biggest mistake of her life.

To Ella's intense relief, Holly had already survived four full days and nights, and Ella herself had managed to keep from becoming too attached to the newborn.

But this evening Deb was leaving to go to a friend's housewarming party. The party had been planned long before the agency had sent her, and Ella waved aside her apologies.

"Go, enjoy yourself," she said. Holly was sleeping peacefully in her cot upstairs. The speaker for the baby monitor lay on top of a pile of magazines on the low, wide coffee table beside the collection of shopping bags that had been delivered not long ago.

With Deb gone, Ella shut the front door and took advantage of the solitude. She was busily manhandling the huge, cut-pine Christmas tree into the corner of the living room, when the doorbell chimed.

She bit back a curse. No choice but to set the tree down…and undo all the progress she'd made in the past few minutes.

Impatient, she wrenched open the door.

Yevgeny stood on the doorstep, every inch the city billionaire, immaculate in a dark, conservative business suit and a white shirt that still managed to look crisp at the end of the day.

"May I come in?"

Before she could respond, he'd brushed past her. Irritation spiked through her at his high-handedness.

Her voice heavy with irony, she muttered, "Sure you can."

He turned and grinned. "Thank you."

The flash of that wolfish smile, the gleam of wicked laughter in his eyes, indicated that he was fully mindful of her irritation. Ella couldn't halt the unfurling awareness that blossomed through her, starting deep in her chest, near her heart and spreading outward in a glow of warmth. Like a flower following the path of the sun.

The man was dynamite.

And she didn't even *like* him. He was obnoxious, arrogant, inconsiderate. So why the melting heat in the pit of her stomach? Why wasn't she recoiling? What on earth was wrong with her? Didn't she have any sense of self-preservation? Ella drew in a deep breath and was instantly flooded with the woody aroma of his aftershave.

God help her if he ever set himself the task of trying to charm her—she'd be in serious trouble!

With a toss of her head, she blew out the breath she was holding and brushed aside the absurd notion.

No threat from him.

Never.

"Holly is sleeping," she said finally as he brushed past her into the living room.

His response had nothing to do with the baby. "You're putting up a Christmas tree."

Did he have to sound so surprised?

"Yes."

Guilt stabbed Ella. She wasn't about to reveal that it was the first time in the five years she'd lived here that she'd done so. Or that most of the reason why she'd ordered a tree to be delivered stemmed from his barbed comments about Holly enduring her first Christmas alone. Becoming aware of the lack of festive cheer in her home had not been a welcome discovery.

"I almost had it in position…but then the doorbell rang." She gestured to where the tree lay. "Now I'll have to start all over again."

He strode across to where the tree lay. "I'll give you a hand and we'll have it up in minutes."

"Shouldn't you still be at work?" She bit off the bit about "making your next million."

He'd walked around to the far side of the tree. Now he shot one immaculate shirt cuff back to glance at a flat watch on his wrist. "Five o'clock. I've had enough for one day—boss's prerogative. I wanted to see Holly."

She refused to let that sentiment tug at her heart-strings.

Instead, she inspected the dark, formal suit he wore and decided it must be French, while she tried to ignore the effect the broad shoulders tapering down to a narrow male waist had on her. "What about your suit? You'll get resin all over it."

He'd reek of a pine forest for months to come. Ella doubted dry cleaning would get rid of the overpowering smell of pine. It would kill that sexy, seductive scent Yevgeny wore so well.

Her lips tilted up in secret amusement.

"What are you smiling at?"

He sounded so suspicious that her smile broadened. He'd find out soon enough. She slanted him an impish look. "Nothing."

"Somehow I don't believe that. You're plotting."

"Gosh, but you have a suspicious mind."

"Do you blame me? I know exactly what you are."

Her smile vanished and her eyes narrowed.

"There's no point in your staying. Holly's sleeping." Ella had had enough of his unwarranted opinions. Now she just wanted him to leave. Before he tempted her to laugh with him…and then he wounded her again. She wanted him gone.

But before she could turn and walk to the front door to show him on his way, he asked, "Have you reached a decision on the new set of portfolios Jo Wells showed you?"

He'd only come to influence—make that sabotage—her decision.

It was her own fault for giving in and revealing she hadn't selected any parents from the first batch of candidates. She'd been overtired…not thinking properly…reacting with her emotions rather than her head. And look where it had gotten her—Yevgeny hounding her.

Ella headed for the door and opened it. "Once I reach a final decision I'll let you know. Then you can decide if you want to stay in touch with the baby and her new family. Thank you for visiting."

Even from across the room, she saw his face fall.

He really had wanted to see the baby, she realized.

The considerations that had led her to update him about progress on the adoption proceedings yesterday returned. Yevgeny was the only blood relative who was showing any interest in the baby; he deserved to be kept in the picture. This would be an open adoption. Jo was insistent that adoptive children needed ties with their birth relatives. Those ties to family helped children grow up secure, with a healthy sense of self and identity.

Ella recognized that she needed to set aside her own antagonism toward the man...and think only of the baby.

As much as Holly needed contact with her birth mother, it would be to her advantage to know her birth father...and her uncle. Having a clear sense of identity would help her to stay intact as an individual as she grew up.

Even though Ella considered Yevgeny Volkovoy to be the most arrogantly selfish man on the face of the planet, for Holly's sake, she had to recognize that his desire to visit Holly was a blessing.

From her position at the door, Ella relented a little. "You can come back when Holly is awake."

But Yevgeny showed no sign of hearing. He'd already shrugged off his jacket and put it on the sofa. "I said I'd help you with the tree."

So he was determined to stay—and ignore her wishes. Why had she ever imagined she might persuade him otherwise? He was accustomed to riding roughshod over other people's opinions.

She didn't want to be stuck alone with Yevgeny making small talk. Nor did she want him putting up the Christmas tree she'd bought for Holly. And she certainly didn't want to start thinking that he was helpful. Or, God help her, indispensable.

"You know, I really don't need—" *nor want* "—your help." All too aware of how much more defined the breadth of his shoulders was with his jacket off, Ella didn't dare to allow her suddenly treacherous eyes to linger on the lean narrow hips, the broad chest clad only in the soft, finest cotton shirt with the top button unbuttoned. Far too tempting. "And don't forget to take your jacket with you when you go."

The sooner he put it back on, the sooner she'd be able to visualize him as a corporate Russian bully.

Leaning on the door handle, Ella shut her eyes to block out the image of him standing in her living room rolling up his shirt sleeves. How was it possible to be attracted to a man she detested?

What the hell is wrong with me?

Six

With her eyes shut and her shoulders bowed, Ella looked more vulnerable than Yevgeny had ever seen her as she leaned against the doorjamb of the front entrance waiting for him to leave.

The last time he'd seen her she'd looked exhausted…but this was worse.

Nothing of the Ella he so disliked remained.

No black suit. Instead, she wore a white, sleeveless T-shirt that clung to curves he'd never known she had, while cropped jeans hugged her legs tapering to slim ankles. The simple outfit only served to underline her fragility.

Yevgeny forgot that he'd come to find out whether she'd looked at the portfolios she'd told him Jo would be dropping off today. He even forgot about his plan to convince her that every parent would be wrong for Holly. Except him.

Instead, driven to comfort her, he padded across the room on silent feet to stand beside her.

She hadn't heard his approach—or, if she had, she showed no sign of it. Yevgeny hesitated. Silky blond hair fell onto her shoulders, the style softer, less sharply defined than he remembered. Her scent surrounded him. Lilacs. Sweet...and elusive.

Slowly, oh, so slowly, he reached out a hand and touched the fine strands where they brushed her shoulder.

She started.

Then her head turned. Behind the large spectacles, her eyes had widened, and the summer sun streaming in through the door transformed the light brown irises to lustrous topaz.

As he stared, her lips parted.

He groped for words that made some kind of sense to fill the electric silence. "What do you want me to do first?"

"Do first?"

From this close he could see her pupils darkening.

All thoughts of offering comfort had rushed out of his mind.

Desire—dark and disturbing—grabbed him by the throat. He tried to respond, but his voice wouldn't—

couldn't—work. But his body was working...in ways he didn't even want to think about. Whoa, this was Ella McLeod of all people. He didn't like her. *And* the woman had given birth to a child last Friday... He couldn't be feeling desire...where was his sense of perspective?

"What do you want me to do with the tree?" he managed at last in a gravelly rasp.

"The tree?" The dazed, startled look in her eyes faded. With her index finger she pushed her glasses up her nose. "Oh. The *tree*."

"I told you I'd help. It's too big for you to try and set up by yourself—and you had a baby not so long ago. You shouldn't be straining yourself."

Her shoulders squared. The veil of fragility fell away from her. "I was doing just fine until the doorbell rang."

Yevgeny pressed his lips together.

That was Ella.

Determinedly independent.

Making it clear she didn't need comfort—or help. Maybe she wasn't quite as vulnerable as he'd thought.

"Do you ever accept help from anybody?" he asked with more than a touch of exasperation, letting his hand drop away. He should be relieved that she'd returned to her usual independent and icy self. At least he could breathe again—and speak. That curious immobilizing spell that had seized his body and paralyzed his vocal cords had started to lift.

Yet he felt a whisper of regret that the moment had passed. God! Had he actually *wanted* to kiss Ella McLeod?

Yes.

The answer shocked him.

He *had* wanted to kiss her, to taste her mouth, to lose himself in her womanliness. Yes, womanliness. There was no doubt about it, Ella was every inch a woman. He would never again be fooled by the lawyer in the black suit again. He'd caught a glimpse of the person—the woman—who lurked behind the legal facade. The lacy night attire. Two pairs of well-used ballet slippers hanging in her bedroom. Even the way she'd held the baby and rocked her in her arms after she'd refused to even look at Holly at first.

She intrigued the hell out of him.

If anyone had told him he'd be hot as a mink in season for lawyer Ella McLeod a few weeks ago he would've howled with scorn. Ridiculous. But now the joke was on him. Only minutes ago he'd been ready to devour her with a desperation that stunned him.

Had he lost all reason?

Could Ella the Icicle really be Ella the Enchantress?

Yevgeny turned away, lest his face reveal the turmoil of his thoughts. Ella was sharp, and he didn't want her recognizing any chinks in his armor that would render him vulnerable to her.

"My parents—when I was younger."

He realized she'd finally answered his question. "They're the only people you accept help from?"

A frown creased her brow. "Probably."

He could see her thinking, trying to come up with other names…and failing. "How about your sister?"

"Keira?" She gave a laugh of astonishment. "She's too young."

"I'm sure you were making decisions at her age."

She shrugged. "Maybe. But Keira always needs help from *me*."

Yevgeny hoarded that nugget of information away, to retrieve and examine later. "What about a mentor…or something?"

Ella immediately shook her head.

He stared then. It was inconceivable to him that she'd never asked for—never needed—help. Even he, who prided himself on his self-made success, had relied on mentors to get where he had so rapidly. How much harder would it have been without the men who had advised him…guided him…helped him?

From slitted eyes he gazed at her with fresh respect.

She'd cleaved a way out for herself—amidst fierce competition—and she'd gained a good reputation. He'd seen the recognition and wary respect her name produced. Ella had done it all by herself.

Without anyone to hold her hand.

"Your parents must be proud of you," he said at last.

"They're very much older."

She'd mentioned that before....

And it didn't answer his question. But it prompted another thought. "Don't tell me you look after them, too?"

In response, Ella inclined her head slightly.

"You do!" He blinked in disbelief. She shouldered the burden of her entire family. "And your sister still comes running to you for everything she needs."

"She always has, but I don't mind. We're sisters, after all." She came instantly to Keira's defense. "Your brother does it, too. I know because Keira told me."

Yevgeny bristled. "I don't have your patience. I told him to make a man of himself." And that decision had probably cost him dearly. For a time Dmitri had torn through the Volkovoy fortune while Yevgeny could only watch. He'd been wild—and irresponsible. A spendthrift and a wastrel. He'd run through everything that was handed to him—and then come back to demand more.

That's when Yevgeny had put his foot down—he'd refused…and demanded that Dmitri come with him to Auckland to set up the new headquarters for Volkovoy cruises.

Dmitri had argued that it was a job for a menial manager. But Yevgeny had refused to bow. Do a job, earn a salary or get out.

They'd quarreled. Dmitri had chosen to get out, screeching off to the smell of burnt rubber and Yevgeny had shuddered with fear and regret. For four days his brother had not returned home. Yevgeny had held vigil and waited for news of the worst.

On the fifth day Dmitri had called and sullenly said he was on his way to Auckland. Yevgeny had thanked the gods and hoped his brother wouldn't do anything recklessly stupid.

Yevgeny later learned he had Keira to thank for Dmitri's success in New Zealand.

Meeting Keira had saved his brother—or maybe it had been being cut off from funding for his lavish lifestyle and being forced to work, to be accountable for his actions for the first time in his overindulged life.

Whatever it was, Dmitri had finally started to grow up.

"I'm very proud of what he's done in Auckland. He's hired premises and sourced some excellent staff."

Behind her glasses, Ella rolled her eyes. "Keira said anyone could've done it. That Dmitri felt it was an insult to be given such a menial task to do."

"At least he didn't screw it up." He flashed her a smile.

"You expected him to," she said after a long moment.

"Honestly?" Her eyes demanded the truth, so he gave it. "Yes, I did."

"How could you think he would fail?"

"I didn't think he'd see it through. He's never had any firm idea of what he wants from life." He paused, then turned the focus back on Ella and her sister. "How can you talk. You don't expect anything of Keira. You still take care of her, sort out all her messes. She never needs to take accountability for anything. You're even sorting out the adoption for a baby she wanted then discarded."

For once Ella had nothing to say. He watched as her mouth opened and closed. Finally she turned away and crossed to where three large store bags sat on the floor. She reached into the closest one and took out a box. She opened it, revealing a tray containing about a dozen shiny, red ornamental balls.

It was a moment of utter emotional devastation.

And Yevgeny felt like a complete toad. It was almost Christmas. It was a time for faith…and family. He'd insisted on helping Ella decorate a tree to celebrate the festivities for Holly—and now he was upsetting her.

That wasn't right. Yevgeny couldn't help thinking that his dearly loved *babushka* would be ashamed of him for ruining Ella's moment of pleasure and forcing her to accept unwanted assistance. She'd already told him to leave—that was what she wanted. If he behaved with the honor that his *babushka* would expect of him, Yevgeny knew he was left with no choice: he must leave.…

He came to a decision. "You don't want me to stay and help you with the tree, so I will leave and come back later when Holly is awake."

With an inward sigh of disappointment, Yevgeny made his way to where he'd abandoned his jacket. But before he could lean down to pick it up, Ella spoke from behind him. "You can stay—if you want."

Yevgeny jerked around in surprise.

She wasn't even looking at him, nor did she sound particularly welcoming, yet his heart lifted.

"Thank you." Gratitude welled up inside him. Before she could change her mind, he moved to the tree and hoisted it up with enthusiasm. "The Christmas tree will look good over here, hmm?"

Ella tucked her hair behind one ear, and shifted her glance to where he indicated. "Yes, I think you're right—that's the perfect spot."

His lips curved in a smile and he shot her an amused look through the gap between two branches. "Good. For once we're in agreement."

She met his gaze. Then, after a moment, she grinned back. "Yes. It would appear we are."

Ella McLeod had dimples in both cheeks.

To avoid the confusion the discovery aroused, Yevgeny ducked down and secured the base of the tree. When he'd safely assured himself that noticing Ella had dimples didn't change anything of great consequence, he finally raised his head again.

"Have you got lights for the tree?" he asked. "They will need to go up first."

Ella dove back into the shopping bags and emerged, waving a box of brand-new Christmas lights with a triumphant flourish. Another smile... and her dimples flashed again.

Blood pumped through his veins.

Yevgeny averted his gaze, and busied himself with taking the box from her hands. Her slender fingers brushed against his large ones—an electric connection. He didn't dare look at her as he broke the seal. Once the lid was open, he lifted the coiled rope of lights out. Immediately Ella crowded closer.

He inhaled deeply.

Lilacs.

Yes, he was in danger of becoming addicted to the subtle scent....

Shaking his head in rejection of that craziness, Yevgeny started to weave the lights through the branches while Ella worked alongside him, making adjustments. He'd never been this close to her for any length of time. It felt curiously—he searched for the right word—exhilarating. When she stepped away to shake out the remaining cable and then went to plug it into the wall socket, he found himself sharply aware of the gray void left in her wake.

A flick of the switch and color lit up the room.

Even Ella's white, cropped T-shirt reflected the rainbow wash of Christmas lights. It looked magical. Yevgeny found himself chuckling at the pretty picture she made.

Ella reached down and switched the lights off. "Now we know they work!"

"Are you always so prosaic?"

She glanced at him through the fan of hair that shielded her face. "Always."

Despite her reply, Yevgeny couldn't halt the spreading of awareness. He considered himself a connoisseur of beautiful women—he'd dated some of the world's best. So why hadn't he noticed how well proportioned her features were? The straight nose, the short delicate arch of her upper lip, and the uptilted curve of her smile all combined to create a striking face.

But he hadn't noticed it.

Until now.

He hadn't bothered to look beyond the dark suits, oversize glasses and abrasive manner.

What else had he missed?

"You have lovely eyes, you know," he said abruptly. "But those hideous glasses you wear do nothing to show them off."

Shock flickered in her eyes, and then a flush stained her cheeks. "Thank you...I think."

"It was a compliment—you shouldn't hide your assets."

Without replying, she pushed her glasses up, then tucked her head down and scrabbled around in the shopping bags again. "I bought decorative balls to hang on the tree."

Ella had changed the subject.

His mouth slanted. Had he really expected a different response? Or was it so hard for her to accept a compliment? He was growing more and more curious about a woman whom he wouldn't have glanced at twice a week ago.

He refrained from pointing out that she'd already opened one box and smiled at her as she continued, "I ordered red-and-silver balls from an online catalog." Ella drew out the second box. "They should look very pretty against the dark green foliage."

He let her off the hook. "My grandmother had a collection of antique glass balls."

That garnered her interest. "Your grandmother? Is she still alive?"

Yevgeny shook his head. "Unfortunately not. She passed away two months ago."

Behind those ugly glasses, Ella's eyes were perceptive. "You miss her."

"Very much—she was a loving woman." Unlike her daughter, his mother. But Yevgeny had no intention to brood about the past.

"She was Russian?" Ella was asking.

"No. She was English." He picked up one of the red balls and hooked the silver ribbon securing it over a branch. After a pause during which he could sense Ella bursting to ask more, he said, "She married my very Russian grandfather after the Second World War—and taught him to speak English. In the process, she became more Russian than he was. The handblown glass decorations she treasured belonged to his family."

"Did she ever return to England?"

"No." But his mother had, taking him and Dmitri with her....

"Was she happy living so far from home?"

It took him a moment to shift his thoughts back to their conversation, and pick up the thread again. Ella was talking about his grandmother.

"She loved my grandfather. Her home was with him." And she'd loved him and Dmitri. *Babushka* had brought some degree of normality into their lives, normality that had vanished once his mother had ripped them away from their father. Without *Babushka* their lives had been barren of feminine affection—because his beautiful mother had had little to spare. Every day Yevgeny remembered his *babushka*'s legacy of kindness. "She was one in a million."

His words hung in the air as they continued to loop decorations onto the branches.

After a few minutes he added, "My *babushka* collected wooden decorations, too. She used to say she liked her tree to be a true *yolka*."

"*Yolka?*"

Yevgeny smiled as Ella tried the unfamiliar word out.

"The traditional tree is called the *yolka*," he told

her. "The first Christmas tree was brought back to Russia by Peter the Great after his travels. The tradition became very popular, until Christmas was outlawed after the 1917 Revolution. It became known as a New Year's Tree."

"That's sad."

"For most of my life Christmas celebrations have been allowed," he said quickly, lest she feel pity for him, "although people had gotten used to celebrating on the first of January, so changing back to Christmas day came slowly at first." Yevgeny changed the subject. "Your family celebrated Christmas?"

Ella hesitated. "Well, we always decorated a tree— and my parents gave us Christmas gifts each year. But they didn't believe in perpetuating the myth of Santa Claus. They were older," she said with a touch of defensiveness when he stared. "And when Keira was young I used to wrap something of mine for her to find on Christmas morning. I'd tell her it was from Santa."

"My grandmother always made sure the family celebrated Christmas," he said, "even in the Iron Curtain years when it wasn't allowed. Although I don't remember that time—I was very young when the prohibition against Christmas was lifted. We would put our tree up earlier than New Year's Day so that we could have a Christmas tree, and we would decorate it with my grandmother's collection of ornaments and tangerines and walnuts carefully wrapped in tinfoil."

When he'd lived in London, even his mother had followed Western tradition and Santa Claus had visited each year. He and Dmitri had at least had the memories of finding gifts under the Christmas tree on Christmas morning—whatever else his mother had done, she had allowed them that small pleasure. What would life have been like for Ella and Keira? To be deprived of such simple joys? Especially when all their friends must've been visited by Santa's sleigh and his reindeer.

And this Christmas Keira would be on the other side of the world.

"Will you be getting together with your parents this Christmas?"

Ella shook her head. "No, we haven't celebrated together for a number of years."

Yes, Ella would be alone.

Not wanting her to see the compassion in his eyes, he turned away and started to hang the silver balls on the tree. But his mind couldn't let go of the image of Ella stoically wrapping her treasures to give to her sister—so that Keira wouldn't miss out on all the fun that went along with Santa. Was that part of the reason Ella seemed so humorless? Had all the fun been sapped out of her young life?

Perhaps…

All the more reason why this Christmas would be different for Holly.

As he made that vow, Yevgeny hung the last silver ball on the tree then stood back to admire their efforts. "Not bad," he declared. "Let's put the lights back on."

"Before I switch the lights on, there's one more item to go on the tree." Ella was unwrapping dark green tissue paper from the object she held in her hands. "The ornament for the top."

The wrapping fell away.

Yevgeny found himself staring at an angel. His first thought was that he would've expected Ella to choose a shiny silver star for the top of the tree. Nothing as personal—and as touchingly humorous—as this angel.

He reached out a hand to touch the angel.

"She's even more beautiful than I thought she would be from the online picture." Ella placed the angel in his hands, then hit the wall switch so that the tree lights came back on again. "She's handmade," continued Ella, as she straightened up. "What do you think?"

The angel wore a long robe of some kind of

shimmery silver fabric. But, as Yevgeny held her up to the light, it was her face that captured his attention. Not beautiful. But full of childlike joy. Chubby and cherubic, the angel's face was brightened by a mischievous smile.

"She's perfect," he replied.

As he reached up and perched the angel on the apex of the tree, Yevgeny couldn't help thinking that in a few years' time, Holly would be itching to be the one to put the angel on top of the Christmas tree.

But Holly wouldn't be here...if Ella got her way.

Green. Yellow. Red.

The wash of light over his face didn't offer any assistance with making Yevgeny's expression easier to read. A mix of pensiveness...and some other emotion that Ella couldn't identify clouded his face.

She hesitated, then blurted out, "Would you like to look through the adoptive parent portfolios that Jo dropped off with me?"

Almost at once she regretted the offer. Already he was frowning. She must be going soft in the head to believe she and Yevgeny could do this without coming to blows. They were polar opposites. They never agreed on anything—this was going to end up in one big battle.

But before she could cast about for a reason to

retract the invitation, the cloud cleared from his face, and he said, "Oh, yes! Perhaps I can finally make you see sense."

He flung himself down on the couch beneath the window and stretched his long legs out in front of him. Crossing his arms behind his head as he leaned back, he looked far too sure of himself.

Taking in the picture he made in his suit pants and white business shirt, together with the stubbled chin and rumpled dark hair, Ella wasn't sure whether to be exasperated or amused.

He looked quite at home…and it would probably take a bulldozer to move him out again.

But the truth of it was, if Yevgeny could see what some of these families had to offer a baby, he might even have second thoughts about his rash and selfish demand to keep the baby himself.

If Yevgeny reconsidered his standpoint, and accepted that adopting the baby out would be in Holly's best interests, it would be so much easier for them all. *If* he was involved in choosing a family for the baby, Holly would come out the winner.

Buoyed up with fresh optimism, Ella collected the five profile files Jo Wells had delivered from the dining table, then seated herself beside Yevgeny.

"Those look heavy." Unlocking his arms from behind his head, he bent forward to lift all but the bottom portfolio from her lap and set the stack on the coffee table in front of the couch.

"They are! They hold the whole life story—or at least the pertinent parts—of each couple." Ella opened the first folder. "This is the hardest part for me, the first photo of the couple together. Look at their eyes. They want this baby, they want Holly."

She paused.

Then, when Yevgeny remained silent, she added, "It's the same with each profile. Every time I have to conquer a surge of guilt before I turn the page."

When he slanted her a questioning glance, she said, "In case I don't choose them."

"I see."

From the look on his face, she could tell that he didn't get it.

"In case I didn't see the plea in their eyes, the desperation on their faces," she said to make it clear.

This time he got it.

She knew it by the shock in his eyes.

Maybe it was the word "desperation" that did it.

Ella turned the page. Then the next…and the next…until she reached the end. "This couple has two sons…they live in an apartment in Auckland City. Both parents are professionals—like me." She looked up to find Yevgeny's eyes already fixed on her. Shock jolted through her. She swallowed, then continued in a slightly husky voice. "Being professionals is good—I want Holly to have a career. But I visualized her having an older sister—and a garden growing up. Kids need space to roam. Two boys and an apartment? *And* their parents working long hours? I don't know. It might mean good money and a comfortable existence, but will the parents be able to give Holly—all of them—enough time?"

Yevgeny shook his head.

She set the portfolio aside and reached for the next one. Leaning back she discovered that Yevgeny had rested his arm along the back of the couch, bringing him so much closer. Tingles danced over her skin as her nerve endings went on high alert. A deep, steadying breath only made her more aware of the musky male scent that clung to him.

Hurriedly, Ella flipped open the folder and concentrated on the first photo.

This time the decision was easy. *No.* The family just was not right. But the following profile was much tougher to look through. The family seemed to tick off all the boxes that Ella could ask for, yet she didn't find herself overcome with enthusiasm.

"They do look lovely—they have a daughter already." She tried to fake enthusiasm as she paged through the file. "A garden. And two dogs."

"Her mouth is too set—she's a witch." Yevgeny

arched forward and pointed at the mother with the hand that was not settled on the back of the couch.

"Nonsense! She's not a witch. She's smiling!" Glancing up to protest, Ella could see the dark stubble on his chin, the hard angles of his cheekbones.

Yevgeny turned his head. Their gazes tangled. "But her eyes are not. And that dog looks like it can't wait to get off her lap."

Ella couldn't breathe!

Feeling crowded, she glanced away…down…and focused on the photo in front of her.

The little girl wasn't smiling at all.

Ella's heart sank. Did that matter? Was it really significant? With a confused sigh she said, "We may be seeing things that don't even exist."

The instant Yevgeny removed his arm from behind her, the twisted mix of excitement and apprehension that had been fluttering in her stomach like a caged butterfly eased. She watched Yevgeny reach for the previous two portfolios, page through them and jab a finger at the family portraits. "In both of these the parents are touching each other."

Ella looked closer—it was true. She glanced back at the third portrait in the folder still open on her lap. The parents sat far apart—a gaping space yawned between them. Despite their smiles neither of them looked terribly happy. "Perhaps it's the pressure—they know how important this is."

"They're supposed to be selling themselves."

"No!" Ella pulled away a few inches to put some distance between them. "They're trying to adopt a baby."

"All the more reason to put the best—the happiest—picture forward."

She wanted to tell him that he was cynical, that he was oversimplifying the matter. But when Ella stared hard at the three faces in the photo, she realized that it didn't work for her. There was no vibe of joy or intimacy.

Ella made her decision and shut the folder with a snap.

She wasn't letting Holly go to this family. "They may be wonderful people. It may have been a tense day when the photos were taken. But that's a no."

She couldn't take that very remote chance of sending Holly to an unhappy home.

A smile lit up Yevgeny's face.

Was that a glint of triumph? Ella stilled. Suddenly his closeness took on a new aspect. Was the enforced intimacy deliberate? Had his comments been staged?

Was she being manipulated by an expert?

She rejected the suspicion almost instantly. She was no pushover.

Then she paused.

Who had the most to gain if she rejected all the families?

The answer came at once.

Yevgeny.

Ella tipped her head to one side and studied him, measuring and resisting the magnetic pull of that sexy bottom lip, the sculpted masculine features and the clear piercing eyes.

Had he deliberately tried to put her off that last family? "You're not asking me if I'm going to change my mind and keep the baby?"

"I know you won't."

The speed of his response took her aback. Ella realized she'd half expected him to try and persuade her not to give up on the child. "Why've you finally decided that?"

His eyes narrowed. Reaction bolted like lightning forks through her. His gaze drifted over her... down...down...sending shivers in its wake...then returned to her face.

Was *that* calculated, too? A deliberate attempt to ratchet up her awareness of him?

Or was she simply far too suspicious?

Ella forced herself to hold his gaze.

"You're not cut out for motherhood." There was distance between them—as wide as the Pacific and many times as deep. He shrugged. "Some women simply aren't."

All the frisson of awareness froze. The delicious moments of understanding beside the Christmas tree evaporated.

She tensed.

The dismissal implicit in his words, in that careless shrug, needled her.

How dare Yevgeny judge her when he didn't even know what made her tick? How dare he assume who she was…and what she wasn't? But she bit back the fierce tide of anger and said instead with quiet force, "What's that supposed to mean?"

Beneath the question lay a vast sea of unspoken pain.

He looked startled at the challenge. "That your career is too important. That you have other priorities." He shrugged again, in that way that was starting to seriously rile her. "It's not unusual not to want to be a mother. I've known other women like you."

He had?

And had he been as clueless about what made those women tick?

Carefully, through tight-pressed lips, Ella said, "I'm starting to think Nadiya had a very lucky escape."

Yevgeny rolled his eyes to the ceiling. "Of course you do."

Then he reached forward and picked the last profile off the coffee table in front of them. "Let's see if this couple is any more suitable than the rest."

Ella let out the breath trapped in her lungs. This time she was determined to open to the front page and fall in love with the family revealed within. This would be it. Then the search would be over, and Yevgeny would have to live with her decision.

But it didn't happen.

The text accompanying the photo indicated that couple had no children. And they requested a closed adoption.

That request unexpectedly rattled Ella.

Badly.

For the first time she realized what it would mean to never see Holly again—or at least not until her baby was all grown up and legally an adult who could request information about the identity of her birth mother contained in the sealed adoption records. To not know what color her baby's eyes turned out to be. To miss out on news about her first day at school. To never see photos of her first school dance.

Ella hadn't contemplated how much comfort having an open adoption gave her. Until now.

She didn't need to read any further. "No."

In the silence that followed, the thud of the folder landing on the coffee table sounded overloud. Ella flinched.

"At this rate you aren't going to find a family for Holly." Yevgeny sounded faintly smug. "You might find I'll be the only choice left."

"Never!" she vowed. That was not an option.

He smirked. "Never is a very long time."

"I'll ask Jo for the next set of files."

"And when all of those families fall short of your rigorous demands, what then?"

Was Yevgeny right? Was it possible that his manipulation had nothing to do with it, that she had set her standards too high? Ella looked away from him and studied the mountain of portfolios through blank eyes, then dismissed his theory.

No, she knew exactly what kind of parents she wanted for Holly.

They were out there.

Somewhere...

Drawing a steadying breath, she pushed her glasses up her nose and glanced across the couch at Yevgeny. "I'll find a family—and you're right, they will be perfect, absolutely perfect, for the baby."

Instead of the usual cocksure arrogance, there was a glint of something close to sympathy in his eyes.

Slowly he shook his head from side to side. "You're not going to find what you're looking for."

"How can you say that?"

"Because I know you, Ella. Better than you know yourself."

Ella rejected that instantly. The man was delusional—he didn't know her. At all. So much for thinking she'd recognized sympathetic understanding in his eyes. All it had been was a different kind of arrogance.

"You're mad," she said.

Yet instead of flaring up in anger as she'd half expected at her accusation, he laughed, showing off dazzling white teeth. His mood had changed again.

"It's day five today. Do you really think you're going to allow yourself to find a family before Christmas if you carry on being this picky?"

It had nothing to do with "allowing" herself. He had that all wrong. When she saw the right couple… she would know deep in her heart that they were the ones. Ella was utterly certain of that.

"I'm not being unreasonably picky," she argued. "I want the right family. I'm not going to rush this."

Even as she spoke Ella could feel the tension starting to rewind tightly in her stomach. Time was of essence. No one understood that better than she did.

She *had* to find Holly a family.

A week from today would be day twelve, the day she could finally sign the consent to adoption. The sooner Holly could start to bond with her family, the better. Yevgeny was right—if she carried on picking apart every family she would only delay letting Holly go to a family who would love and cherish her.

But on the other hand…it *was* almost Christmas.

How could she push the baby away before Christmas? She paused.

Why not…

Before she could stop herself her mind traveled down the forbidden path. The anguish she'd expected didn't come.

Yes, why not?

Ella came to a decision.

"I don't have to find a family before Christmas. I'm going to wait until after Christmas. That way Holly can spend her first Christmas here." Fearing the blaze of triumph she was certain Yevgeny's face would reflect, her gaze flicked to the corner dominated by the giant tree with its merry flashing lights.

The red-and-silver balls gleamed warmly.

The right family would emerge after Christmas.

Once she'd taken down the Christmas tree that Yevgeny had helped her put up this evening…and finally said goodbye to the baby…she would have plenty of time to reflect—and come to terms with how her life had been unexpectedly changed. And perhaps she would even follow Jo's advice and attend grief counseling.

For now she would take it one day at a time.

In the meantime, she'd take photos—make an album for the baby to take with her to her new life. That way Holly would one day be able to look back and see where her life had started.

And Ella would be satisfied that she'd done everything she could for the baby.

Because Yevgeny was right: she wasn't the kind of woman who wanted to be a mother. She was enough like his own mother to terrify him.

She was determined to choose someone better for Holly.

Seven

Seated behind the desk in her office, a legal pad open in front of her, Ella gazed sympathetically at the young, heavily pregnant woman on the other side of the desk. When Peggy had arrived to start work early this morning, she'd discovered a pregnant, tearful Pauline Patterson waiting in the lobby for the law offices to open. Taking in Pauline's red-rimmed eyes, Ella could see why her paralegal had been worried about the young woman and why Peggy had wasted no time in summoning Ella back to work.

"You're certain divorce is the course of action you want to take?" she asked Pauline.

"I can't afford a lawyer, but my sister said if I didn't retain one my husband would take me to the cleaners."

A few more questions elicited the fact that Pauline Patterson's sister seemed to have a lot of opinions about the marriage—yet some of the problems that were plaguing the couple didn't sound insurmountable to Ella. Especially given the sadness in Pauline's eyes when she spoke of leaving her husband.

Carefully Ella asked, "Have you tried couples counseling?"

Pauline shook her head. "No. My sister said I needed a lawyer—to show Ian I meant business."

Ella ignored the sister's views and explained, "Through the courts you're entitled to six free sessions. I strongly recommend that you try counseling first." Ella couldn't stop herself from glancing down at Pauline's swollen stomach. "It's a good idea to exhaust all alternatives first. Divorce is stressful for everyone…and it can be very final. Sometimes there is no going back."

Fear flared in Pauline's eyes. "I still love Ian. I don't really want to get a divorce—I want to sort this out. My sister says this is the best way to get his attention."

"He's not listening to you?"

"His friends are more important to him than me or the baby." There was a doleful note in the young woman's voice. "I miss my mother—she's back in

England. Now that I'm pregnant, I need help." Tears rolled down Pauline's cheeks.

"Have you told your husband you need more help—that you miss your mother?"

Pauline shook her head. "No. His mother and my mother both said we were too young to get married. I've been determined to prove them all wrong. To show everyone—even Ian—that I wasn't too young."

Ella asked a few more questions that revealed that money wasn't a problem. Although both Pauline and Ian seemed to shop more than they should, Ian had a good job with prospects of another promotion soon. Nor, to Ella's relief, was he verbally or physically abusive. It appeared this was a case of both of them needing to grow up quickly now that they had a baby on the way, and learning to talk and listen to each other better.

Coming to a decision, Ella said, "Before you go further down the road with a divorce, why don't you talk to Ian about your unhappiness? I suggest that you both go to counseling and visit a budgeting service. If Ian refuses to go, I think you should take advantage of the sessions for yourself."

Ella reached into a drawer for business cards for a couple of counselors who worked with the court, and another card for a local budgeting service.

She smiled at the young woman as she handed the cards to her. "Sometimes, when you spend more than you earn, financial worries can put a lot of pressure on a marriage—particularly if there's a baby on the way. And if Ian is out with friends all hours of the night when you're tired and pregnant, resentment can breed. These people may be able to help you. If they can't, and you still feel certain that dissolving your marriage is the only way forward, come and see me again. We will put a plan into action."

Pauline glanced down at the business cards she held. "You really think this will work?"

This was a question to which Ella never had a good enough answer. "There are no guarantees. But at least you will know in your heart that you tried everything before you decided that divorce was the only solution. And that will help you when you start the road to recovery. You'll have fewer regrets."

Over the years Ella had learned that often parties who consulted with her determined to secure a divorce wanted nothing more than to be pointed in the right direction to save their marriage. Not in all cases, but enough for her to know that six sessions of counseling were worth trying first.

As Pauline thanked her, tears of hope sparkling in her eyes, Ella's lips curved up into a small smile, and she couldn't help wondering what Yevgeny would say if he saw her now—hardly the hotshot lawyer out to destroy every marriage in town for an outrageous fee.

* * *

Yevgeny took in the tearstained face of the young woman exiting Ella's office as he stood aside to let her pass. Then he entered Ella's workspace, shut the door behind him—and pounced. "You're doing her divorce?"

"That's none of your business!"

Ella's light brown eyes were cool. She stood behind the barrier of a highly polished wooden desk, clad in one of those black power suits he'd come to hate.

"She's pregnant!" The angry words ripped from him.

"That doesn't mean anything. There are times when divorce is the right thing—even for a pregnant woman."

"And what about the baby's father? What if it's not the right thing for him?" Blood pounded in his head. Everything he'd come here to say had evaporated from his mind. Now he could only think about another divorce…another father deprived of his sons. *His* father. "What about the father's rights?"

"Everything in a divorce is negotiated."

"Not if the woman lies." It was a snarl. "Not if she manipulates everything and everyone to get sole custody, and bars her husband from ever seeing the children…I mean, the child," he corrected himself quickly, as he stalked to the front edge of the wooden desk. Ella still stood on the other side. She didn't seem to have noticed his slip of tongue, as she watched him, unmoved. "Both father and child lose then. I ask you, is that right? Is it fair?"

"Yevgeny, it's my job to make certain—"

"Your job is to be a divorce lawyer."

"Family lawyer," she corrected.

"You broker agreements, which keep boys from their fathers and wait like a vulture over a kill."

"*What?*"

She drew herself up, which wasn't much higher than his shoulder, Yevgeny knew. Her eyes blazed gold fire at him across the expanse of the polished desk.

"I don't do anything of the kind! Divorce is hard on everyone. It's my job to make the arrangements workable after a marriage ends. And that means taking the children's needs into consideration from the very beginning. Sure, the spouses are often furious with each other, but it's part of my responsibility to make sure that the party I'm representing is aware that their children take priority. I don't try to prevent the father's access to his kids—unless there's reason to do so. Violence. A history of abuse." She shrugged. "My job is not always pleasant."

"I'm not talking about instances of domestic

violence." Yevgeny refused to back down. "I'm talking about women who manipulate you—and the judge." His voice was thick, his Russian accent pronounced. He drew a deep, shuddering breath and forced himself to relax.

He'd arrived at Ella's house earlier to visit Holly—and discovered Ella had abandoned the baby to return to work. He'd been outraged. He'd come here to tell Ella what he thought of her—not to be dragged into the past.

Her brow wrinkled. "Are we talking about a specific case here?"

He looked away. His stomach tightened. For a moment he could smell the long-forgotten musty smell of another legal office with its wooden-paneled walls and leather chairs. He could see the never-forgotten triumph in his mother's smile as she rose to her feet to shake the lawyer's hand. It had been three years until he'd seen his father again, and only because his mother had walked out of the fancy house his father paid a fortune to maintain, leaving her two sons alone in it. The housekeeper had called his father to advise that his mother had gone—she couldn't have cared less.

When he looked back at Ella, her head was tipped to one side as she inspected him. The brown eyes no longer flamed, they'd warmed to the pale gold of honey behind her glasses. "Did you have a child taken from you in the past?"

He'd never heard that soft, sweet tone from her before.

My God. She felt pity for him! No one ever felt that kind of emotion for him. *Never.* It rocked Yevgeny. He shook his head in a jerky motion, rejecting the very idea. "This is not about me!"

"Isn't it?" Ella stepped around the desk and came toward him. "Are you sure?"

This wasn't about him…this was about…about— *His Holly.*

He could feel every muscle in his body growing increasingly taut with every step that brought Ella closer. He wanted her to stop. He didn't want her coming near enough for him to pick up on her lilac scent. He didn't want her kindness. Not until he could examine why her sympathy caused him to crack wide open inside.

Yevgeny struggled to marshal the anger and outrage that had driven him here. He'd rather remember the side of her he detested—the human icicle, the mother who wanted to send the child she'd given birth to away and abandon her without a second thought.

That was the woman he never wanted near him.

And he knew the easiest way to keep that woman—
and her questions—at bay....

"What did you advise your young client?" he
barked out. "To wangle as much from her husband
as she can? To lie to get sole custody?"

Pausing, one foot in front of the other, Ella halted,
and Yevgeny exhaled a silent sigh of relief.

Mission accomplished.

Then she said, "You can't expect me to answer
that. Any advice I give is subject to legal privilege.
But I can tell you that before proceeding with
divorce action, I often suggest to clients that they
try counseling—"

"Airy-fairy stuff." Yevgeny waved a dismissive
hand. "No help at all."

"Or get budgeting advice," she continued evenly
as if he hadn't interrupted. But her eyes sparkled
behind her spectacles. "I'm sure a financially savvy
man like you would appreciate the wisdom of
that."

One dark eyebrow shot up. "Budgeting advice so
that these women can afford your usurious fees?"

"No!" For the first time Ella sounded annoyed.
"Budgeting advice to help them save their
marriages!"

He took in the anger on her face. He was angry,
too. This was not going to help his position with

Holly. Yevgeny let out his breath. "This is not why I came. I will call you when we both have had a chance to simmer down."

Given their previous confrontation, the last person Ella wanted to see when she walked into her home the following evening was Yevgeny. She still had not "simmered down" as he had put it.

To make matters worse, he looked totally at ease sprawled across the carpet of her living room, his gray satin tie loosened, shirtsleeves rolled up and his hair ruffled. Holly lay on her back beside him, looking perfectly content, her bare legs kicking in the air, while the Christmas tree sparkled merrily in the background.

It was all very cozy and festive...a scene from a Christmas card...and Ella felt like a complete outsider in her own home.

"Where's Deb?" she demanded, stopping in front of Yevgeny.

"I told her to take a break while I'm here."

His high-handedness annoyed Ella. Deb reported to her, not to her nemesis. It was something she would have to discuss with the nanny.

Then Ella told herself to lighten up. It was Friday evening, she wanted to relax...but his presence nixed any chance of that.

Holly gave a squeak, and Ella instantly dropped to her knees beside her. The baby appeared to be fascinated with her own hands. She gave another high-pitched shriek.

Ella's heartbeat steadied.

Of course there was nothing wrong!

Except that she was hovering too close to the baby....

She shifted and glanced away.

Straight into Yevgeny's curious eyes.

It was a good time to remember that she hadn't forgiven him for likening her to a vulture circling a kill yesterday.

Which led her to one of the many questions that his visit to her offices had raised....

"I never did find out what you were doing at my offices yesterday. I take it you didn't simply arrive planning to call me a vulture?" Ella raised a questioning eyebrow.

He looked discomforted. Sitting up, he said, "I ordered in dinner—I thought you might enjoy not having to cook tonight. You could give Deb the entire evening off."

"Then I'd have to look after the baby instead of cook," she pointed out, not sure that she liked the fact that he'd walked in here and taken over her life.

She held her breath, waiting for him to accuse her of all the motherly shortcomings he usually did.

A furrow creased his brow, and she tensed. He surprised her by saying, "I intended to play with the baby. I thought you might want to relax. Keira once said you like to take Friday evenings easy."

Ella blinked.

He was trying to be considerate?

Was that possible? Her gaze slid to Holly. The baby was wriggling her fingers and making cooing sounds. She looked wonderfully content. It shouldn't be too difficult for Yevgeny to look after her.

"You ordered dinner in?" she asked in case she'd misunderstood.

"Yes, Italian."

That really got her attention. She loved Italian food. How did he know that? Had he pumped Peggy for information about her yesterday? Or had he been cross-examining Deb? Another thought struck her. . . .

"Should I consider this an apology for your rudeness yesterday?"

A flush seared the high, Slavic cheekbones. "The food is from La Rosa."

The diversion worked. "I didn't know La Rosa does takeout—much less that they deliver."

"They don't."

So he was pulling out all the stops. "But you convinced them?" His sheepish nod confirmed it. "Who told you it's my favorite restaurant?"

"Keira."

"You spoke to Keira today?"

"No—she mentioned it a while ago."

"Before they left?"

"Yes." The word was dragged out of him.

What interpretation was she supposed to put on his reluctant confession that he'd remembered— and acted on—something Keira had most likely mentioned in passing?

Ella grew impatient with herself. It probably meant nothing more than that Yevgeny Volkovoy had a frighteningly good memory.

Something she'd be wise to keep in mind.

True to his word, Yevgeny tended to Holly. He even helped Deb bathe and change the baby before the nanny left. He played with the baby, waving toys and rattles to stimulate her interest. Before she could become too caught up in watching Holly interacting with her uncle, Ella excused herself to express milk from her aching breasts for the baby's next feed and to enjoy a soak in a bubble bath before the meal arrived.

By the time she emerged, dressed in comfortable

skinny jeans and a T-shirt, wonderfully relaxed and scented from her fragrant hot bath, Yevgeny had set her dining table for two and, more miraculously, gotten Holly off to sleep. The handset from the baby monitor lay on the table.

Ella was impressed by his efforts—even though her eyes lingered on the second place setting.

Yevgeny intercepted her gaze. "I am staying. I want to assess whether La Rosa's cuisine lives up to your high recommendation. And I have something I wish to ask you. But I think I hear the food arriving. Let's eat first."

To Ella's delight the meal was excellent—well up to La Rosa's high standards, even without the ambience of the restaurant setting. Even better, Yevgeny graciously declared it to be among the best Italian he'd eaten in a long time.

"As an apology, that meal was most certainly acceptable." Ella set down her dessert spoon after savoring the last spoonful of tiramisu and smiled at him.

Rather than take umbrage at her gentle ribbing, he laughed, but once his laughter died away, an awkward silence settled over the table.

Ella broke it first. Pushing her spectacles up her nose, she said, "Are you ready to tell me why you came to see me yesterday?"

He picked up his half-full glass of red wine and sat back in his chair. "I was annoyed that you'd gone back to work. I intended to confront you."

"You have no right to question my decision. My practice is my livelihood. I don't meddle in your business." Ella leaned forward, determined not to allow him to push her around. For once, the big Russian had the grace to look abashed. "Besides, I made it clear from the outset that I wouldn't look after the baby. I'm giving Holly up for adoption. I don't want to make what is already a difficult situation more difficult by bonding with her." Even by expressing her milk to feed the baby, Ella suspected she was becoming closer than she'd ever meant to be to Holly. Inside she could feel her muscles tensing and the all too familiar anxiety that she took such pains to conceal rising. The sense of well-being that the soak in the tub and the delicious meal had instilled was rapidly ebbing.

"I understand."

"Then why your annoyance yesterday?"

He didn't answer, instead swirling the glass and appearing to be enraptured by the deep ruby glow of the wine. Then he looked up, and the illusion of contentment shattered. His eyes were full of turmoil. "I understand now. I spoke to Jo Wells earlier."

What had Jo said? Ella sought his eyes for answers.

But found none to justify the panic that flared inside her.

Jo couldn't have told him anything. Because not even Jo knew.

Unless Keira had told her...

Ella blocked out the possibility of such a devastating betrayal.

"The way Jo explained your decision not to bond with the baby made me realize that it wasn't an act of neglect or selfishness."

Her teeth snapped together. She'd been trying to get that through to him. But he listened to a stranger? "Thanks!"

"She also said that you wouldn't be forsaking Holly—that you intend to keep in close contact with her. She told me that you were always adamant—even when Keira and Dmitri planned to adopt her—that Holly should know that you were her tummy mummy."

Despite her outrage, it was so incongruous to hear him use that term for surrogacy that Ella almost smiled. "It's always been important to me that there should be no deception in this kind of situation—it only hurts the child." She shuddered inwardly as she looked away.

If he only knew...

When she glanced back, it was to find that

Yevgeny was swirling the wine again, staring into the rich, red depths.

It must be hard for him to face the fact that he'd seriously misjudged her—and admit it. Many men would've shirked this. Maybe it was time to cut him a little slack.

"You can drink it," she assured him to lighten the mood. "It's a good wine—gold medalist, in fact."

That brought his gaze back to her. "I didn't think you would poison me."

This time it was Ella who laughed. "What makes you so sure?"

"You uphold the letter of the law. I don't see you as breaking it. I'm starting to realize you have plenty of integrity."

The unexpected compliment warmed her.

Her lips tilting up, she said, "Flatterer!"

He shook his head. "No, it's the truth…which I appear to have managed to miss."

"While we're on the topic of truth, what was really going on in my office yesterday? I asked you if you'd lost custody of a child in the past. Tell me about your child, Yevgeny," she invited softly.

A mask dropped into place.

He smiled. But no hint of humor lit his eyes. It was as though a dark thundercloud hung over him. Ella shivered, no longer sure she should pursue this line of questioning. There was pain there…and something else.

"What child? I've never been married."

Ella slanted him an old-fashioned look to lighten the mood. "I didn't think you of all people would believe you had to be married to get someone pregnant."

He chuckled. "Very funny!"

She wrinkled her nose at him, and decided to probe a little more. "So what was it all about?"

"What do you mean?" he stalled.

"There was something else going on."

"You're imagining things."

She stared at him for a long moment. His mouth was flat, there was no hint of the humor that had lit his eyes only seconds before she'd started pushing. "I don't think I am. What's more…I think it has to do with a lawyer—but not me." She thought about her own life, about what had caused her to develop her prickly, reserved shell. "Did a woman do a real number on you?"

He laughed, and she detected a palpable tension beneath the careless sound. "Never!"

"She was a lawyer, wasn't she?"

He laughed again.

This time with relief, Ella suspected. Okay, so she wasn't quite there yet, but she was definitely on the right track. She was certain of it when Yevgeny said, "You're making too much of this—"

"Because you never let anyone in," she interrupted. "No one gets close enough."

His reaction was recognizable. She did the same thing. It was what she'd been doing ever since she was nineteen. She guarded her emotions zealously, only letting Keira past the barricade of her defenses.

"What did she do?"

"Stop trying to psychoanalyze me."

"Why?" She leaned across the dining table, and rested a hand on his arm. Beneath her fingers his flesh was firm, the muscle taut. For a moment she marveled at her brazenness. "Am I getting warm?"

"Warm?" He recoiled from her touch. Ella let her hand fall. The skin stretched across his cheekbones until his face resembled a death mask. "You're as cold as ice."

She got the double meaning at once. Yevgeny considered her cold. It hurt.

Ella swallowed and looked away, determined not to let him see what his words had done to her.

What did it matter that he thought that she was as cold as ice? He wasn't the first to think so, and he wouldn't be the last. It was what she'd wanted, wasn't it? She'd cultivated a cool, distant manner to keep men like him at bay. She certainly didn't want him to feel she was approachable, or God help her, receptive to his compliments and flattery and the advances that would inevitably follow.

Or did she?

That thought was the most horrifyingly painful of all.

Escape became a necessity for survival.

"I think I'll go and check to make sure the baby is sleeping." She stumbled to her feet before he could comment on her sudden maternal urge. "I'm sure you're ready to go. You can close the front door behind you."

It was only after she heard the front door softly close long minutes later that Ella realized that she hadn't discovered what Yevgeny had wanted to ask of her.

Eight

Yevgeny wasn't certain of his reception when he rang the doorbell to Ella's home on Sunday morning. So when she finally opened the door and the warm summer sun fell on her face, he experienced an unfamiliar, giddy surge of relief.

"You never did say what you wanted to ask me on Friday night." Behind her spectacles, her honey-brown eyes were wide with wariness. "I expect that's why you're here today. Or have you come to see Holly?"

It shouldn't surprise him that she'd guessed what he was doing here. But it did. The way in which she was so attuned to his thoughts, his actions, should've driven a stake into his heart. He didn't need Ella of all people possessing the ability to read his mind.

There was too much that was private—and some information was not his alone to share.

Yet, instead of bolting in fear as he had on Friday night, he stood his ground.

Nor did he take refuge in half-truths and claim that he'd only come to visit Holly, although the baby did play a big role in his presence here today. But, to be fair, he'd played with her when he'd passed by yesterday. Ella had been out. "I wanted to ask you if you would come with me to look at a house I'm thinking of buying," he said, deciding that directness would be the best policy.

Whatever she'd been expecting, clearly, it hadn't been that.

"You're buying a house?"

He nodded. More than a house, a home. For him… and Holly.

With the sun playing across her features Ella looked warm and approachable. For a moment he had a vision of…

Then he pulled himself together.

What was he considering? Was he mad?

He tried to get a grasp on his thoughts…and answer her so that she wouldn't get a whiff of the crazy notion he'd experienced. "It's time. The penthouse apartment has never been more than a place to sleep after a long day's work. I want a building with space around it. A garden. And I'd like a woman's opinion on the house I've seen."

Ella rested one arm against the doorjamb, blocking his entry. "Why not take Nadiya— Why me?"

He gave her a disbelieving look. "Do you think Nadiya would want to come and look at houses with me after the humiliation of our last encounter?"

He didn't want to take Nadiya—or any other woman. It had to be Ella. No one else would understand....

"You haven't seen her since?"

The question jolted him. "Nadiya?"

"Yes, Nadiya."

He shook his head.

Ella hesitated. "I suppose I could join you. Now would be better than later. I'd planned to prepare for a meeting on Monday. So, as long as you give me a few minutes to get ready, I'll come. Holly is taking a nap. I'll need to tell Deb we're going out so that she can get her ready."

"It might be a good idea to leave Holly here."

At the surprised look she shot him, he added reluctantly, "My Porsche is a two-seater." It was becoming clear to him that, along with a new home, he was going to have to purchase a new car, too.

"We can take my car...it's a station wagon," she said wryly.

That amused Yevgeny. Ella didn't have dogs or children yet she drove a station wagon? He kept the observation to himself. "We'll take my car and leave Holly at home. That way the visit will take less time." And as much as he adored the baby, this morning he wanted Ella's undivided attention. It would be easier to assess her gut response to the house without the baby around to distract her. "I'll call the Realtor to arrange access."

"You'd better come in while I get ready." She stepped away from the doorjamb to let him pass, and tossed him a prim smile. "I won't be long."

As Yevgeny followed Ella indoors he told himself it was going to be okay—everything would work out. The sunny morning. Her smile. The fact that Christmas was fast approaching.

All augured well.

He could sense that Ella was beginning to weaken.

As Yevgeny pulled the Porsche to a stop, Ella's breath caught in her throat.

Nestled amidst sprawling gardens, the house was not a multimillion-dollar sculpture comprised of a series of post-modern boxes.

It was a jewel of a home.

With wide lawns and big leafy trees, it cried welcome to a family—not a bachelor billionaire.

Yevgeny unclipped his seat belt and turned to her. "I like the feel of this place. What do you think?"

What did she think? She loved it. But…

Ella stared through the tinted windshield trying—and failing—to imagine Yevgeny living here all by himself. "It looks…big."

"Three stories, garage for half a dozen cars, several reception rooms, a home cinema, an indoor heated pool, staff quarters—and six bedrooms," he recited. "But that's not what interests me."

He climbed out the sports car and came around to open her door before she could ask what *did* interest him—if not the sheer impressive scale of the residence.

"Come."

Ella followed Yevgeny along the path that led up to the house.

Her emotions were all over the place. Why was Yevgeny considering buying such a house? He already had a penthouse apartment—from what she'd heard it was extremely luxurious. Why did he need a house, too?

Unless…

For Holly?

But Ella was not ready to face what the answer to that might mean. For the baby. For her. For everyone. Instead, she paused under the spreading, twisted branches of an old pohutukawa tree, and said, "Ah, a real, live New Zealand Christmas tree. It's made for a tree house."

His gaze followed hers to the beautiful branches loaded with bunches of red flowers. "I'm afraid I know little about tree houses—Dmitri and I never had one."

"This calls out for one." Squinting upward, Ella continued, "In fact, there's enough space for a playhouse up there. It would need to be furnished. Chairs. A table. Kid-size crockery. Keira and I had a tree house growing up—we spent hours in ours."

"What did you do?"

"We held tea parties. And played dress-up. And one summer we even made lemonade from the lemons that grew in the garden and opened a stall." She turned her head to discover a slightly stunned expression in Yevgeny's eyes.

Finally he said, "Then I'll know who to call on to attend to the decor when the time is ripe."

She smiled, but didn't acknowledge the burgeoning certainty that the playhouse would be for Holly. Yevgeny had no intention of disappearing from the baby's life.

It seemed like a huge amount of trouble to go to for a child he would only see for periods agreed to by her adoptive parents. Unless…unless he still believed he could convince her otherwise?

No.

She'd made her position crystal clear—she wanted the baby to go to a family…. Yevgeny would have to accept that once she found the right parents for Holly.

And it was her choice.

Not his.

Hers.

This house was for him—not Holly. Although Ella recognized it would be lovely for Holly to have such a fantasy place to visit from time to time.

He was looking past her at the old tree with its low, sweeping branches crowned with red flowers. "Now, I can see that that bough would be perfect to support a swing."

"A swing?"

Switching his attention back to her, Yevgeny gave her a crooked smile. "Holly would love it."

So it *was* about Holly…not just him.

For a moment Ella allowed herself to imagine him pushing Holly on the swing on a warm summer's eve…she could even hear Holly's laughter ringing out.

Then she pulled herself up short.

No.

This house wasn't for Holly…it was for Yevgeny.

Primarily because his penthouse apartment had grown too small for his requirements. Better she keep her mind on task.

"Let's look inside," she said briskly.

The Realtor waited in front of the white front door at the top of the stairs. A smartly dressed woman with dark hair and hungry eyes, she smiled at Ella. "Mrs. Volkovoy?"

Good grief! "No." Ella felt herself flushing. She shouldn't be here. She was starting to feel like an imposter. "I'm not his wife—I'm a lawyer."

The Realtor's gaze arced to Yevgeny. "You didn't mention you were bringing your lawyer."

"Ella is not my lawyer," said Yevgeny through clenched teeth

"Oh." The Realtor's curious eyes darted between them. To Ella's relief the woman didn't ask any of the questions that were clearly burning to escape. "Perhaps I should let you browse—and we can talk afterward?"

"Perfect." Yevgeny gave a grim smile. "We'll catch up later."

Ella couldn't help wondering what the hell she was doing here as she rushed to keep up with Yevgeny's long stride.

"Oh, wow."

Yevgeny stopped at the sound of Ella's breathy

exclamation. She was standing in the middle of the living room, staring out the wall of glass sliders leading to a long veranda with a backdrop of verdant gardens and sea beyond.

"One could spend the entire summer living on that veranda," she said, transfixed. Then she gestured to the sleek fireplace in the end wall. "But in winter the fire would make it warm and welcoming inside."

"There's a hot spa at the end of the veranda to make winter even more pleasant," Yevgeny told her.

"How fabulous."

"And a kitchen and dining area made for entertaining on the other side of the dividing wall," he added. "The home theater and wine cellar are downstairs. But come and look upstairs." He wanted her opinion on the bedroom and playroom where Holly would spend most of her time.

"This one. What do you think?" Upstairs he led Ella eagerly to the second bedroom.

As Ella scanned the bedroom from the doorway, taking in the bright sunny light spilling through the high arched windows, he saw her surprise register.

"But this isn't the master bedroom. You wouldn't occupy this room." Her eyes held a question as they met his. "This is for a…" Her voice trailed away.

Yevgeny could see the realization dawning as she entered. He headed in after her.

The room was decorated in shades of rich cream and pale blue. A bed with an intricate white ironwork bedstead was piled high with a collection of soft toys on a patchwork comforter, setting the girlish tone. Overhead, a chandelier winked in the sunlight. There was a window seat beneath the arched windows with space for picture books.

He could imagine Holly seated there paging through her favorite book as she grew up. Perhaps he could even ask Ella to help him furnish the room in a similar style once the house was his.

"This…this room is for Holly, right?" Ella sounded choked up.

Yevgeny came to a stop in front of her. "Yes. Do you like it?"

She shrugged her shoulders helplessly. "What can I say? It's perfect."

For that heartbeat they were in perfect accord, no hint of the animosity that had dogged their relationship since their first meeting. Yevgeny held his breath, loath to say anything lest the instant of harmony shatter into jagged shards of discontent. Seconds passed, and they stood drenched in warm sunlight in the house Yevgeny wanted for a home.

Deep in his chest hope started to build. Ella was starting to see things his way.…

At last he moved.

Her eyes squeezed shut.

"Ella?"

At the questioning lilt of his voice, her lids lifted. And she looked straight into his eyes. Yevgeny felt a physical jolt. He was so close that he could see the shades of velvet brown and glittering gold. Desire flared. And something more…something new and fresh.

Again the crazy vision he'd glimpsed on her doorstep earlier and dismissed rose up. It was cemented with how right…how happy…Ella appeared to be in this setting.

Ella fit this place…

He bent his head. His lips met hers…pressed… waiting.

Hers parted.

The kiss deepened.

Closing his own eyes he sank into the softness that was Ella, a softness he'd never expected to discover, and concentrated on imprinting the instant in his memory to pull out and analyze later. To make sense of the inexplicable. For now, he simply absorbed the feel of her body against his. The warmth. The womanliness. The sweet, lilac scent that was the unique essence of Ella.

Finally, when his head lifted, his breath was ragged and he felt dazed and disoriented.

To his enormous dismay, Ella recovered first.

"Well," she said, the bright flush on her cheeks already starting to fade, "I don't think we need to take a look at the master suite after that."

Ella glanced at her watch.

They were back downstairs, standing on the spacious veranda protected from the sea breeze that ruffled the tops of the great trees that flanked the house.

"Need to be somewhere else?" Yevgeny drawled. He leaned against the balustrade, blocking her view of the well-kept gardens below. "Or are you in a hurry to leave?"

Ella looked up at him.

The sun splintered in the gold of her eyes, blinding him for an instant.

Yevgeny blinked.

Ella was speaking, and he struggled to focus on what she was saying.

"No, I was simply thinking that if this was a weekday I'd be in my office working." She made a sweeping gesture with her arm. "Solving other people's problems and missing out on all this beauty."

It was a relief to break away from the spell of her golden eyes, to swing around and follow where her arm indicated, out over the vista of the gardens to the azure sea and the hazy horizon beyond.

The crazy feeling was back. *Affinity.* A vision of him and Holly and…

He drew a deep, shaky breath.

"I have a proposition for you."

"A proposition?"

Ella lifted a hand and nudged her glasses up. If he'd known better he might have thought she was apprehensive. But this was Ella—she didn't have an apprehensive bone in her body. "Play hooky with me tomorrow."

That gave him twenty-four hours to decide how to broach the topic they most needed to discuss.

Holly…

"Pardon?" She blinked at him.

"Take the day off—we can take Holly out for the day." It would be easier with the baby there. "And enjoy the December sun and fresh summer air. It's almost Christmas, take some time out."

Her brow creased in a frown. "I have a meeting."

"Can you postpone it?"

She shook her head slowly. "It's important."

"Holly is important—nothing else comes close. In five years' time will you even remember what this meeting is about? Because Holly will still be important then."

Ella pushed her glasses up her nose. "I can't—not tomorrow."

"No one else can do it?" he persisted, frustrated. This was important—too important to be overshadowed by work.

Ella shook her head again. "I'm the only one who knows all the fine details."

His frustration bubbled over. "Then you have a problem—you need to learn how to delegate."

"To whom? No one else—"

"Can do the job as well as you?" He raised an eyebrow.

Ella nodded slowly. "I suppose that's what I mean."

"Then you have two problems—maybe more. You've surrounded yourself with the wrong people, you've failed to train them adequately, you don't empower your staff by giving them responsibility. Or all of the above."

"None of the above." Ella's teeth snapped shut. She gave him a "take that" look.

Yevgeny narrowed his gaze. "Then you're guilty of bad planning."

She made a peculiar sound, and stalked to the end of the veranda, where she stood with her back to him, looking out over the garden. Her shoulders were stiff. In the pause that followed Yevgeny found himself watching her…anticipating her next volley. Until he caught himself.

He padded to where she stood, and her shoulders stiffened. This was not what he wanted. "Ella—" He broke off as heels clicked on the tiles behind him.

The Realtor had returned.

Ella still hadn't responded. Yevgeny sighed. "You go to your meeting. I'll take Holly to the park."

To his surprise, she didn't object.

"Are you going to put an offer in on this house?" Ella asked too softly for the Realtor to hear, her back still to him.

He nodded, suddenly tired of the dance around the truth, and then realized she couldn't see his acknowledgement. "Yes," he said. "This will be my home."

Once back at her town house, Ella made a hasty escape on the pretext of checking on the baby, the memory of his unexpected kiss in that wonderful house still numbing her mind.

Ella was in turmoil. Joining Yevgeny for a romp in the park with Holly had been beyond her.

Ella knew that Yevgeny was going to pressure her again.

To try and convince her that he would be the best thing for Holly. She was so confused. Yevgeny offered none of the qualities she wanted in the family who'd adopt Holly.

He was a bachelor. A type-A billionaire. He wasn't even in a stable relationship. Sure he had a stable full of centerfold supermodels at his disposal, but that was hardly the same thing....

Yet, as she entered the nursery, Ella found herself wondering whether she'd leaped from the frying pan into the fire.

Holly was awake, gurgling happily to herself in the white cot.

Coping with Yevgeny was child's play compared to this....

"She's just woken," Deb told her from the depths of the rocker where she sat surrounded with the Sunday newspapers. "I swear she knew you'd come home. I might go to the kitchen and warm a bottle for her."

"Thank you." Moving slowly across the room, Ella paused beside the cot and glanced down at the baby inside.

Holly moved her head...then chuckled.

Ella told herself it wasn't possible. The baby was too young to be laughing. And she hadn't spent enough time with Ella to form a bond. The baby couldn't possibly recognize her...could she?

Yet Ella couldn't resist.

She bent down and laughed with the baby, an ache in her heart. Her breasts felt hot and tight. Ella tried to convince herself that Deb's mention of the milk bottle had stimulated the need to express. That was better than the danger of the instinctive age-old maternal response at the sight of her child.

Holly kicked her bare legs in the air, and Ella grasped the perfectly shaped little foot. Her fingertips brushed the soles, and the baby crowed with delight.

"You're ticklish! I've discovered your secret." She leaned closer and whispered, "Never fear, it will be safe with me."

Warmth rose within her, fierce and unfamiliar. What spell was Holly weaving about her? Why could she no longer think of the baby without a smile curving her lips? How was she ever going to let the baby go?

This was precisely what she'd fought so desperately to avoid. This...this emotional tug that went all the way to her womb.

As if feeling her straying attention, the baby gurgled and pumped her legs. Ella smiled again but this time there was a tinge of sadness in the smile.

She would not be privy to all Holly's secrets as she grew up. That would be a role taken by someone else…a woman who could love Holly with all her heart, a mother who wasn't crippled by fear—and pain.

"I'm going to find you the best mother in the world, I promise."

She was so intent on the exchange with the baby, that she didn't sense the arrival of the man in the doorway. Nor did she see him hesitate before exiting, a stormy frown darkening his face.

The Porsche purred as it swept through the bends along Tamaki Drive. On the right, white sails fluttered in the wind in the bay as locals enjoyed the Sunday summer evening, while across the sea the menacing volcano of Rangitoto Island slumbered.

So Ella was going to find his baby the best mother in the world?

Yevgeny braked and geared down for the next curve. He slowed as a pack of cyclists came into sight, throttling back the powerful engine to a throaty roar.

Ella was still determined to give Holly away to strangers. Despite everything he had done to show her that Holly belonged with him….

Watching as one cyclist cut to the center lane, he dropped farther back. A moment later the bikes were bunched up together again, the cyclists in their bright attire pedaling furiously.

Maybe not *everything*.

The time had come to use all the weapons in his armory.

And that meant confronting his brother.

It was not the path he had ever intended to take—for his brother's sake. But Ella's talk of transparency on Friday night had set him thinking.

Ella was right about one thing: Holly came first. The bond—because that's what it was, a fast, blood bond—that tied him to the baby was as vital to him as breathing. He would not risk losing her.

Tonight, when he announced to his brother what he was going to do, there was a very good chance it was going to cost him their relationship. But Dmitri had Keira.

And Holly had no one…except him.

He already knew his actions were going to alienate Ella. He'd hoped to gain her cooperation by letting her see how much the baby meant to him, but it was finally starting to sink in that Ella would never be swayed from her viewpoint. She was not prepared to recognize what he had to offer Holly.

He had a claim to the baby—one that would secure his place in her life. He had the money and resources to fight Ella and win temporary custody. Up until now, the only thing that had stood in his way of using the brute force of legal muscle had been his brother—or, more accurately, his brother's pride.

The Porsche swung easily into the next curve. Ahead, the group of cyclists had spread into a single file, and he nosed past.

In the previous ten days he'd grown to know and love Holly. He could not walk away. Yevgeny was all too conscious that tomorrow was D-Day, as he'd come to think of it. It would be his last chance to convince Ella that Holly belonged with him. Because the day after tomorrow, Ella would be legally able to sign a consent to allow Holly to be adopted by another couple. Once that was done, the decision would be final.

Sure, she'd said she was going to wait until after Christmas. But Yevgeny could not risk the danger that Ella might change her mind.

Then all would be lost.

Holly would be lost to him.

Forever.

Tomorrow was his best chance.

Tonight he would contact Dmitri far away in Africa to let his brother know of the decision he had made. Because he could not do what he had to do without letting his brother know. He'd left it too long already—because of his misguided confidence in his ability to convince Ella to come round to his point of view.

Time was fast running out....

Nine

The meeting dragged on.

Ella doodled on the legal pad in front of her and wondered what Yevgeny and Holly were doing in the park. Yevgeny had taken Holly alone, giving Deb a sizable block of time off for the first time in over a week. Now Ella was fretting. Had she done the right thing letting Yevgeny take the baby out alone? Of course she had. He was the baby's uncle—he deserved some sort of relationship with Holly. The next worry popped up. Had Deb packed the bag? Would Yevgeny have remembered to take a bottle? To put sunscreen onto the baby's fair skin? Her gaze slid to where her cell phone sat on the conference table beside her legal pad.

She could call him....

"What do you think, Ella?"

The question wrenched her out of her reverie. Ella set her pen down and forced herself to focus. This was important. *But would it be important five years from now?* Yevgeny's lecture came back to her.

Ella gazed around the table. Two unsmiling executives dressed in pin-striped black suits stared at her. The older executive was the CFO, the younger was the corporation's legal advisor.

Would the outcome of this meeting be important in five years? She considered the radical thought. Work—any work—had always been important. But this time? Ella wasn't so sure. Originally she'd viewed this meeting as an opportunity to gain a toehold in bankruptcy law, and add another specialty to her expertise. But it didn't fit with the rest of her family law practice. She was no longer sure she wanted to do the company's work—she didn't even like the CFO. She'd handled his sister's divorce and received the referral. It had sounded like a great opportunity.

But she didn't want to spend her days filing bankruptcy suits.

So what was she doing wasting precious time on this? Where had her ideals of building a quality practice doing work she loved gone? What was she doing representing corporate sharks? And for what? More money? More prestige? Longer hours?

Was it worth bargaining her soul for?

"Will you be able to do the work?"

"Sorry?" Ella struggled to grasp the implication of the CFO's question. Was he doubting her legal ability? Both men were watching her across the polished expanse of the table. Her stomach knotted. She'd missed a crucial part of the dialogue. Now she was floundering. "I missed the last bit."

"I heard you had a baby." The CFO's tone was patronizing. His gaze dropped to the legal pad in front of her, then lifted to meet hers. His expression said it all. She was losing her edge; her femininity was the problem.

Ella found herself flushing. She resisted the urge to cover the doodles, to deny every thought she read in his face. Then she caught herself.

Why should I feel ashamed?

She had been daydreaming…imaging Holly and Yevgeny out in the sunshine, then fretting about all the things—important things—Yevgeny might forget.

It had taken Holly less than twelve days to change her life.

For the first time in years she was focusing on what she wanted. Evaluating. Choosing.

What had happened to her dreams? When had her desire to only take on work she wanted to do become hijacked by visions of wealth and power? That had been the whole reason she'd left the large, city practice where she'd been a rising star. She'd wanted to be able to take cases that interested her— refuse those she didn't wish to do. Not have her days...weeks...years dictated by billable hours.

It had worked out. She earned a good living...she had a retirement plan...her town house was paid off...she worked for herself and was answerable to no one.

She wanted for nothing.

But along the way she'd become more ambitious. Her schedule had become crowded.

There was no time left for...Ella.

When had she last taken a vacation? She'd always loved movies. When had she last taken the night off and gone to watch a movie and share a tub of popcorn with Keira or a friend? And, for that matter, when had she last actually met up with any of her friends? Ella couldn't even remember. Most of the people she socialized with these days were her work colleagues.

"I don't think I'm the right person for the job," Ella found herself saying. "But I have a colleague who might be a perfect fit. Let me call your office later with his contact details." There was immense satisfaction in watching the CFO sputter for words. Ella rose to her feet, and gave the pair her most gracious smile. "Thank you so much for considering me. I do appreciate it, but I think Mark Stanley will be a much better fit for your company."

And she was going to rewrite her business plan to focus on the work she did best—and enjoyed most. But first she was going to see if she could find Yevgeny and Holly.

She was going out to play in the park.

Yevgeny spotted Ella approaching long before she reached them. There was something about the way she moved that had clued him in that it was Ella when she'd still been a speck in the distance.

"You were worried about the baby. You thought I'd screw up." Partly annoyed by Ella's inability to give up control but also pleased that she'd been worried enough about the baby to come to the park, Yevgeny grinned at her from where he was sprawled on a picnic blanket on the grass in the shade of an ancient oak.

"I wasn't worried."

Yevgeny didn't believe that for one minute. "So why did you come?"

She glanced away. "I thought it would be nice to be outside on such a lovely day."

He snorted in disbelief.

"I did. Honestly! I—"

She was talking so fast that Yevgeny found his grin growing wider. "Slow down!"

Ella stopped talking abruptly and gave him a sheepish smile. Her dimples appeared. Then she sank down beside Holly, who was sound asleep on the blanket. She touched the baby's cheek with one finger and Holly made a snuffling sound.

Ella quickly withdrew her finger. "I don't want to wake her just yet."

"How did the meeting go?" he asked.

"Fine." Her face tightened.

Not fine, then. His good humor faded. "There was a problem?" He couldn't help remembering his criticism of her priorities. It made him feel guilty.

"No." She paused. "Not really."

"There was a problem." There was no doubt in his mind.

She turned to face him. The bright gold eyes were dulled by specks of unhappiness. Something was bothering Ella. And Yevgeny was surprised by the wave of protectiveness that swamped him.

"What went wrong?"

She hesitated. "Nothing. The meeting went fine. *I* was the problem."

Stretching out beside Ella and the baby, he propped himself on his elbows. Keeping his eyes intent on her face, he asked, "What do you mean?"

"It's hard to explain." She shrugged.

"Try," he prompted, sensing quicksand ahead.

"I'm not sure I understand myself." She looked away.

Yevgeny sensed this was not the time to push her. Above them the wind rustled through the leaves. He could hear blackbirds chirruping.

"Something has changed."

The admission surprised him. "You were treated different than usual?"

She shook her head. "That's not it. It's me—I've changed."

He studied her, seeking signs of the change she was talking about.

The wind caught at her hair. One hand brushed a recalcitrant strand back behind her ear. Except for a mussing from the wind's touch her hair was sleek and styled. The black business suit Ella wore was smart—even though by virtue of sitting on the picnic blanket she was showing far more leg than the designer had ever intended to be revealed in the office.

His eyes traveled down the length of leg encased in sheer stockings. Until he reached her feet. She'd kicked her shoes off. Already scraps of grass clung to the stockinged soles of her feet.

She might look the same…

But he would never have imagined that Ella he'd known before sprawled across a picnic blanket in a suit, her hair wind-tousled, her shoes abandoned.

She *had* changed.

"If you want the truth, I like the change."

Her eyes widened. "You can see it?"

He found himself leaning forward. "You're more relaxed—not so uptight."

"Uptight?" She drew away. "I'm not uptight!"

The quicksand deepened. He drew a measured breath. "I meant that as a compliment, not a criticism."

The look she flicked him was laden with uncertainty. An uncertainty that bothered him far more than he cared to admit. Had he been so critical of her? That she had to examine everything he said for hidden motive? Yevgeny didn't like that thought at all. He always considered Ella opinionated and judgmental. Had he been every bit as bad?

Leaning forward, he brushed the grass cuttings from her stockings.

She wiggled her toes and jerked away. "Don't!"

Acting on instinct, he grasped her foot and pulled it back to him. Then, on a wicked suspicion, he tickled the sole of the foot now resting against his leg.

She gave a shriek of laughter that she quickly bit off.

"You're ticklish." The discovery delighted him.

"Very." She glanced at the still sleeping baby, then mock frowned at him. "Don't you dare!"

"I never could resist a dare."

Or the temptation of revealing this unexpected side of Ella....

She convulsed with laughter as his fingers descended. "I haven't even begun," he protested.

"No, no." But she was laughing.

So he tickled more.

She writhed on the blanket, breathless with mirth. Her body rolled up against him, and Yevgeny went still. He had only a moment to make the decision... it was no decision. His fingers trailed away from her foot, his touch firming as he stroked along her leg.

Her laughter faltered, and her head turned. She must have glimpsed the intent in his eyes because her breath hooked in her throat.

The sudden silence was deafening.

Her lips moved. "Yev—"

Before she could protest he shifted his body and slanted his mouth across hers.

Then he waited.

She made no sound, no move rejecting him.

She gave a little gasp beneath his lips. Then her mouth opened like a flower.

Then a growling wail broke the tension.

"It's Holly, she's awake!" Ella pushed at his shoulders. "Let me up."

Yevgeny rolled away onto his back, one arm flung across his eyes. The baby sure picked her moments....

"My God. Anyone could have seen us." Ella's breath was coming in shallow gasps. "What was I thinking?"

"You weren't thinking...." Yevgeny lowered his arm to gauge her response "You were feeling."

"What's that supposed to mean?" Ella picked up the baby. "That I don't feel? That's what you believe?" She clasped the baby to her chest, rocking her. "That I have no feelings?"

It was hardly the time to confess that he'd considered all her feelings to be entombed in ice. Nor could he lie. He settled for, "I didn't know you."

"So you jumped to conclusions instead of trying to find out more."

There was nothing he could say to refute her statement.

"So much for being someone who doesn't react on impulse."

Having his own words flung back at him was no more than he deserved. He tried not to flinch. "I still believe that is the best way—even though I am perhaps not the best example."

"Well, at least you're honest."

"And you're generous to concede that. Thank you." Her shoulders sagged as she let out a deep breath. She hitched the baby higher.

He reached awkwardly forward. "Let me take her. She must be heavy."

"I can manage."

His arms fell away. For the first time he took in how comfortable Ella looked holding the baby. This wasn't a picture of a woman who couldn't wait to get rid of the child in her arms. Ella looked…maternal.

Surprise jolted Yevgeny.

He blinked. Looked again. Ella still looked perfectly at home. He waited for Holly to regurgitate the bottle he'd given her before she'd gone to sleep over Ella's formal suit. But that didn't happen. Instead, Ella continued looking down at the baby cradled in the crook of her arm with a curiously content expression.

Yevgeny couldn't concentrate on anything except Ella.

Every time he turned his head, those golden eyes ensnared him. The rose-tinted mouth that was so much softer than he'd ever envisaged. The Ella he was discovering behind the professional dark suits and efficient manner was very different from what he'd built her into.

So much more.

Her humor. Her rounded, infectious laugh. The love for her sister. The way her eyes softened like melting honey when she looked at Holly and thought no one was watching.

She even possessed a degree of sensitivity and self-awareness he'd never expected—she knew she was changing.

Like one of his *babushka's matryoshka* dolls where every layer opened to reveal something different. Something unexpected and new. Another layer that entranced him even further.

His chest tightened.

Yevgeny shook his head to clear the confusion. He must be dreaming…having such thoughts, such feelings about Ella.

But Ella was right about one thing: he knew far too little about her. And that was something he intended to remedy.

Starting now.

"What's your star sign?"

Her head lifted, and her attention switched from Holly to him. "My what?"

"Your star sign."

"I heard you, but I can't figure out why you'd want to know. Surely you don't follow astrology?"

He shrugged. "All women know their star signs." Some that he'd dated consulted their horoscopes every day. He couldn't understand why she was fussing about it.

"Because they hope that some vague prediction of good fortune will get them something that usually takes plenty of work."

His mouth quirked up. He suspected that assessment fit a couple of women he had known. "You're talking about finding a husband?"

"No! I'm talking about career and the financial benefits that come with hard work."

"Ah, I should've known." He had known. Of course that's what she meant. But he couldn't resist teasing her. She rose to the bait so beautifully. Every time.

She cast him a suspicious look. "I don't read my daily horoscope."

He didn't grin. "I imagine you read the financial pages."

"What's wrong with that? At least I have a better idea where the real financial advantages lie."

He held his hands up in surrender. "I'm not arguing with that logic."

"Really?" She tipped her head to one side. "Are you saying you actually agree with me?"

"You're surprised?"

Her lips curved up into a smile that attracted his attention to her mouth—her very kissable mouth, a mouth he was rapidly becoming addicted to. But with Holly now awake he had no chance of exploring that new obsession anytime soon.

Better to focus on getting to know what other surprises Ella had in store....

Holly chose that moment to squeak and reach out a hand to tug at Ella's bracelet. As soon as she had Ella's full attention the baby started trying to blow raspberries.

"Oh, Yevgeny, look!"

She laid the baby back down on the blanket and spent the next few minutes playing peekaboo. Holly was wide-eyed with interest.

Ella was laughing.

And Yevgeny knew he needed to get to know this woman better.

"What's your favorite color?"

She stopped giggling at Holly's attempts to blow raspberries and blinked at him. "Why?"

"Just answer."

"Why do you want to know?"

The familiar frustration rose. "Are you always this suspicious?"

"Of you? Yes."

"Why?"

"Because you're not the kind of man who engages in careless conversation. There's always a reason behind everything you say. But I can't figure out why you'd want to know what my favorite color is."

He lowered his voice to a purr. "If you tell me gold, I can tell you it matches your eyes. Or if you say rose, I could compare it to the flush on your cheeks."

Her cheeks flamed. "Why would you want to say such things?"

"You are a beautiful woman—when you allow yourself to be."

"Is this part of the same conversation about my not having feelings?"

He took her hand in his and turned it over. "Rounded nails. Your nails are carefully tended."

She snatched her hand away.

"Wait. I haven't finished." He retrieved it from where she'd laid it back in her lap. "No nail color."

"I'm sorry that displeases you."

"It doesn't displease me, but it tells me plenty about you."

"What? That I'm not trying to capture a man's attention?"

"There are many ways to capture a man's attention. Painted nails are only one." He stroked the back of her hand. "Your skin is soft. That's very attractive. You take care of it."

Her lips parted, but she didn't utter the words that he could see bubbling. Instead, her breathing quickened.

God. He was only touching her hand....

Yevgeny let it go. "When is your birthday?"

"Why? Do you want to read my horoscope? Or do you want to buy me a present?"

"Perhaps—but it would be difficult to choose. I don't know you very well."

"You don't get your assistant to pick out gifts for all your women?"

There was a buzzing in his ears. "Are you saying you're one of my women?"

She paled. "Of course not!" She fussed with the bottle that Holly had discarded. "I can think of nothing worse."

"Nothing?"

Her gaze dropped to the baby and he knew she'd

gotten his point. Giving Holly up for adoption was far, far worse than being his woman—or the next step, having a child with him.

Then he spelled it out, "It would be easier to give Holly away, would it?"

Ella went white, and for the first time he noticed the sprinkling of bronze freckles across her nose. "It won't be giving her away. She'll be going to a family who desperately wants a baby to love—and I still intend to see her from time to time." She paused. There was a peculiar light in her eyes. "If you really want to know, my birthday was Friday before last."

It took him only a moment to make the connection. "The day Holly was born."

There was no way in hell he could say any more.

Ella didn't look at the baby on the blanket beside her. Instead, she wrapped her arms around herself. "I better get back to work. I have one more appointment before I'm done for the day."

"What do you mean you don't care?" Frustration soared as Yevgeny changed the cell phone to his other ear and tried to ignore the crackle that distorted his brother's voice. Yes, it must be the crack of dawn in Africa. Without a doubt, he'd woken his brother out of a deep sleep. But he wasn't sorry. He was too relieved he'd finally made contact, after almost twenty-four hours of trying. He'd pulled the Porsche over to try calling—and gotten lucky. "But you never wanted anyone to know you're sterile. You swore me to secrecy."

Dmitri mumbled something to the effect that Keira already knew—and that was all who really mattered.

Of course Keira knew!

How else had Holly been conceived with Yevgeny's donated sperm?

Which Ella didn't know. She still believed Dmitri was Holly's biological father. And Yevgeny had been so confident that she'd ultimately allow him to adopt Holly without the need to air Dmitri's tragic secret.

He'd sure been wrong about that.

Yevgeny was relieved that the baby wasn't here to experience his raised voice. He never wanted her associating her daddy with anger. He'd left her with Deb only ten minutes ago; soon he would be back at his penthouse.

"But you were so adamant about it," Yevgeny gritted out. Hell, if he'd known his brother had become so casual about who knew about his sterility he'd have told Ella yesterday at that bewitching house. Or earlier today at the park.

He'd had the opportunity.

A year ago it had been a different story altogether... then Dmitri hadn't wanted anyone—except Keira—

to know the truth. He appeared to have forgotten all about that.

"Yevgeny, it was you who was so uptight about it." Even over the distorted line he could hear his brother's protest.

"*Me?*"

That wasn't true. His brother had always been deeply embarrassed about the sterility that had resulted from his contracting mumps when he was young. During his teen years it had been a shameful secret as he roared around wildly with gangs of girls to prove his virility. Even now the memory of those days, the fights he'd had as Dmitri leaped from one disaster to the next made Yevgeny shudder.

"Yes. You thought it made me less of a man. A sissy."

"I *never* said that!" He struggled with an impotent sense of growing outrage.

"But you thought it."

Never! "Where the hell did you get that screwed-up idea from?" he growled.

"You."

Yevgeny sucked in a breath, counted to ten. Outside the Porsche the street was alive with people hurrying home at the end of the day. "Then you read me wrong."

"*You* were terrified about it getting into the papers.

You didn't want anyone to know you'd donated sperm in case *Babushka* found out."

That part was true.

"Maybe I overreacted about that." It was a huge admission to make. Again he was guarding his brother. His grandmother's one shortcoming in life was that she'd always been very conservative—and tended to be too outspoken and hurtful at times. "*Babushka* was probably a lot tougher than I give her credit for being. But it was more than that. I was terrified of the paparazzi stalking you. The stories in the gossip rags would emasculate you." And shame his brother further.

Too late he realized what he'd said. Silence crackled down the line.

"Dmitri?" No answer. More loudly he demanded, "Dmitri?" He was thankful that the Porsche was soundproof. The woman wheeling a pram past the passenger side didn't even turn her head.

An angry grunt told him his brother hadn't hung up.

"I'm sorry." The words came with difficulty. "That was tactless." And that instinct to protect his brother had been there all his life, started by his mother calling Dmitri a crybaby.

"Tactless?" This time he heard a laugh. His shoulders sagged with relief as Dmitri continued.

"My never-wrong brother admits he has been tactless?"

"That's how you see me? Never wrong?" Yevgeny knew he sounded incredulous, but dammit, he'd never heard Dmitri going on like this. Like a sullen child. How long had this resentment been simmering?

"You've always taken charge of everything—there was never any space for me to do anything—you had it all under control."

It sure as hell didn't sound like he had it all under control now! "Dmitri, is everything okay?"

"I'm fine. Better than I've ever been in my life."

"What does that mean?"

"I'm discovering what it means to be myself."

"But you always were yourself." Yevgeny couldn't understand any of this. It was starting to feel as if he'd barged into one of those online gaming sites his brother habitually frequented—a dark, confusing alien parallel universe.

"No." His brother denied. "I was drifting. I wasn't myself. I was living in your shadow."

Yevgeny started to take issue with that, and then stopped to consider what Dmitri was saying. Perhaps he had tried to force choices on his brother, but he'd done it for Dmitri's own good. He had worried Yevgeny with his wild behavior, spendthrift ways, fast cars and equally fast women. Had he unconsciously adopted his mother's attitude that his brother was weak?

His brother was talking again. Yevgeny forced himself to concentrate—to really listen. "Keira's calling. I have to go help in the clinic."

"The clinic?"

"It's a health clinic. Run by volunteers. A nurse comes once every second week—mostly to attend to vaccinations and refer more serious cases to the nearest doctor two hundred miles away. I did a first-aid course in Auckland, so I'm working there."

"You've done a first-aid course?" Yevgeny couldn't keep the surprise out of his voice. "I didn't know."

Dmitri said, "You also don't know that I'm tossing around the idea of going to university to study to become a doctor."

"A doctor?" Yevgeny decided that he must be dreaming.

A laugh came down the line. "There's a whole wide world out there, *braht*—you should see it one day."

But right now Yevgeny needed permission from his brother. "So I can tell Ella?"

"Yes. Keira never wanted to keep it from her. But I thought you didn't want anyone to know your brother was less than a whole man. So I convinced her it was better this way."

Oh, Christ. "I've made a right mess of it, haven't I?"

It didn't matter what he had or hadn't thought. His relationship with his brother was clearly far from healthy.

After a moment his brother came back with, "It's not your fault alone. We always seem to talk at cross-purposes."

"That's going to change," Yevgeny vowed. And his brother wasn't the only person with whom he had a communication issue.

The realization, as he ended the call, was not a pleasant one.

But it had to be faced. His interaction with Ella had been based on quick judgments and half-assed opinions from the start.

No wonder he'd stood no chance of gaining her consent to adopt Holly. But he intended to change that. It was time he put all his cards on the table, and told Ella the truth.

Ella's last appointment took longer than she'd scheduled.

When her cell phone rang, Ella glanced at the caller ID. Yevgeny. Her fingers hovered over the face of the phone. Finally she pressed the button to kill the call and let it divert to voice mail, then looked back at the man sitting in front of her.

Jerry Foster was at the end of his tether.

Two weeks ago he'd received divorce papers. Like many of Ella's clients, he hadn't even known his wife had been unhappy. Yes, Lois had nagged him to change his workaholic habits a couple of years ago; and, yes, she'd asked him to join the tennis club and play doubles two nights a week but he'd been too busy with the business. He'd told her to find another doubles partner. He'd thought the problem was solved.

Until two weeks ago.

Now he was in a spin. His wife was demanding custody...occupation of the marital home...and worst of all, Jerry was starting to suspect that her new doubles partner was more to her than a fellow tennis player. What Jerry wanted, he'd told Ella, was not a divorce. What he wanted was to keep his wife and kids.

Jerry wanted his life back.

He was ready to do whatever it took to restore his marriage. But his wife wasn't playing ball.

"Why won't she talk to me?" He jabbed his fingers through messed curls, the gold of his wedding ring glinting in the office lighting. "I was doing this for her—for us," he amended.

Jerry owned a multimillion-dollar investment

company. It generated enough income to more than meet the family's needs for years to come.

"I wanted her—our family—to be cared for," Jerry was saying. "Not like my mother. My father died when I was ten, a heart attack, and my mother had to scrub toilets to put food on the table."

"Did you ever explain this to Lois?" Ella asked gently.

Jerry looked at her as if she were an alien from another planet. "Of course not. I didn't want her to feel sorry for me. I always played down my roots. My mother died the year before I met Lois—there was no need for her to know all that sordid stuff."

"Do you think she would've loved you less if she'd known about your background?" Ella wasn't a therapist but she'd seen similar versions of this sorry tale played out too many times to count.

A feeling of déjà vu settled over her.

"No!" He looked shocked. "She's not like that. She's the kindest woman I ever met. That's why I love her so much."

The confusion in his eyes made Ella feel like crying.

Jerry didn't need a lawyer—he needed someone who could teach him how to communicate with his wife!

A knock sounded on the door. A moment later Peggy peered around the door frame.

"I have Mr. Volkovoy on the line. He says it's urgent."

Ella gave her cell phone a sideways glance. There were three new messages since she'd killed that call a few minutes ago. Her heartbeat picked up. Holly. Had something happened to the little girl? And if so, wouldn't she have heard from Deb first? Drawing a deep breath she told herself not to jump to conclusions. "Do you know what the matter is?"

"He wouldn't say. But he did admit it wasn't a medical emergency."

Holly was okay!

Ella silently blessed her assistant's unflappable common sense.

"Tell him I'm with a client. I'll call him back in about ten minutes when our meeting is done."

Peggy nodded. "I'll let Mr. Volkovoy know."

Yevgeny found himself pacing the vast black marble floor of his penthouse as he waited for Ella to call him back.

He wasn't sure what childish urge had compelled him to insist it was an emergency. He wasn't used to women not being available to take his calls—and being left to cool his heels. Yet he suspected he'd behaved badly. How often had he been annoyed by women calling and insisting that trivial matters were crises that needed his immediate attention? How often had that led to him backing out of the relationship?

He didn't like the idea that he was acting in a similar, irrational fashion.

In truth, the very idea scared the hell out of him.

Not that he was in any kind of relationship with Ella....

When Ella's call finally came, it came through on his cell phone. He leaped on it.

"You were looking for me?"

Her voice sounded warm and welcoming. He stopped pacing. Something in him responded and he felt the tension that had ratcheted up during his conversation with Dmitri slowly uncoiling. "Yes, I was." He searched for words.

"I called Deb. She says Holly is fine. Is it Keira—has something happened?"

There was a note of fear in her voice now. Yevgeny squeezed his eyes shut. God. Why hadn't he foreseen that his stupidity might cause her to worry needlessly? He opened them again and stared out the wall of glass but, for once, the spectacular view failed to register. "No, no, nothing to do with Keira."

He hesitated.

No, filling her in over the phone about his conversation with his brother was precipitative. He'd talk to her…face-to-face…as he'd planned. Now wasn't the time to go off half-cocked; too much was at stake.

"Then what's wrong?"

"Nothing's wrong."

He shifted his feet. He could feel himself coloring. He felt like a total idiot. It was not a familiar feeling. Against this backdrop he was going to break the news of what he planned to do? He had to pull himself together, or else he was going to end up alienating Ella forever. And that would not be in Holly's best interests.

But the edginess wouldn't leave him. "Uh—I have to go to a charity function tomorrow night."

Today was D-Day.

Was he taking too much of a risk, leaving it until tomorrow? Even though Ella had said she'd only make a decision about Holly after Christmas?

"Yes?"

There was confusion in Ella's voice.

"I accepted several weeks ago." While he'd still been dating Nadiya. "For myself and a partner. I was wondering whether you would be prepared to come with me?"

His grip on the cell phone tensed.

"You want me to go on a date with you?"

Yevgeny couldn't tell whether she was annoyed or amused. Nor did he want to point out that technically they'd been on two dates already—one he'd orchestrated at her home with food from La Rosa and the second at the park earlier.

"That's what was so urgent?"

The disbelief in her tone made him writhe.

Because he wasn't being truthful.

Turning away from the glass wall, he started to pace again. "The organizer called me to get my partner's name for the table lists— I needed to let her know."

"Urgently?" she asked pointedly.

"Yes— The function is tomorrow." He'd forgotten all about taking a date. Hell, finding a woman had been far from his thoughts these past couple of weeks. The only female that filled his head had been Holly—and Ella. But she didn't really count.

"Why me?"

He hesitated again. He'd reached the silver-and-black open-plan kitchen. He swung around. Then stopped. He drew a deep breath, and let it out slowly. Then he leaned back against the kitchen counter.

God, he was becoming more and more tangled

in this deception—even though he'd planned to be honest and put an end to it all.

"Because I can't believe you haven't got someone else in your little black book you could call," she blurted out when he didn't answer.

Yevgeny found himself grinning. "I don't have a little black book."

She clicked her tongue. "The contacts list in your phone, then."

How to admit that none of them stirred his interest enough? His mind skittered away from the terrifying specter that thought raised—the only person he wanted to ask was Ella. Because that had to be wrong. It could never be true.

She was prickly and defensive. Not his type.

She reminded him of his mother.

Or did she? Flashes of Ella laughing with Holly. Of how she looked at the baby. Of her gentle cloying concern for her sister. Of her care for her elderly parents.

For the first time he realized that his assumption was quite untrue: Ella was nothing like the woman who had given birth to him—and then deserted him.

Ella would never desert Holly.

She planned to stay in touch with a baby who was never meant to be hers. She only wanted what she considered the very best for Holly—even though Yevgeny didn't share her views.

"Why me?" she asked again.

"Because you would probably have held it against my proposed adoption if I turned up with a beauty queen from my contacts list."

There was a silence in response to his facetious reply.

Then she said, "I don't think—"

"Please," he said abruptly, kicking himself for not holding his tongue.

"You could go alone, you know."

"I probably will. It's a charity event—I'd feel bad not showing up." With a sigh, he said, "You would've enjoyed the ballet."

"Ballet?"

Yevgeny held his breath.

"Which ballet?"

A vision of two pairs of ballet slippers with faded satin ribbons danced before his eyes. He had her! A smile curved his lips up. *"Giselle."*

He heard as she sucked her breath in. Finally she said, "I'd love to come with you to the ballet."

Ella set the phone down, terminating the connection to Jo Wells.

The day she'd been waiting for had arrived.

Yevgeny was due to pick her up in—Ella glanced at her watch—two hours. She still had to beat the rush-hour traffic home, see that Deb had handed Holly over to the night caregiver, express milk for Holly's night bottle, shower and glam herself up. Now Jo was on her way, too.

Of course, everything always did happen at once.

The social worker had identified a couple whom she believed met every one of Ella's criteria. A professional couple who'd already adopted a two-year-old girl, they had a very good relationship with their daughter's biological parents and grandparents. Their home was located in a rural suburb of Auckland, less than forty minutes drive from where Ella lived. The property abounded with pets and ponies, with a garden that led down to the sea.

They'd flown through the police checks. The family offered everything and more.

Jo was ecstatic. She was bringing the profile file for Ella to view immediately.

The family was so perfect that Jo's biggest concern was that the biological mothers of two other babies currently waiting for adoption might choose this family. But Jo had said that the family was more than happy to let Holly spend Christmas with Ella— if that was what Ella wanted.

Ella knew she should be experiencing profound joy. But she could only feel the heaviness of dread.

When she examined the dark source of that heaviness she concluded that deep down she'd been secretly hoping that Keira would come to her senses and contact Ella to claim the baby. Was that why she'd been stalling? Was that why she'd vetoed every other couple?

Why she'd been so critical of every other solution available to Holly? Even the option Yevgeny offered? She closed her eyes. She didn't even want to think about the house Yevgeny was going to buy. Every nook and cranny of her memory of that place was infused with imaginary visions of Holly running across the lawns, Holly playing on the swing Yevgeny intended to build, Holly curled up in the window seat while a fuzzy feminine figure read her a story—

But this would be an open adoption. No reason why Holly would not still have that... She would visit Yevgeny. This family clearly welcomed full participation for the biological family.

There was no reason to hesitate. Ella knew she had to breach the barrier and take the final, irrevocable step.

But she had to face that it wasn't a case of Keira coming to her senses—Keira had made her own choice. She wanted to find herself—she wasn't ready to become a mother. Keira was a grown-up. Ella could no longer make her decisions—live her life—for her. Keira had already had twelve days to change her mind.

But she hadn't.

Ella knew it was time to stop clinging to a thread of hope that had already snapped.

She had to stop putting roadblocks up. This state of limbo was stressful for everyone. And it was unfairest of all to Holly— Every day that passed was taking away the opportunity for the baby to form a strong relationship with her new mother. Ella knew she had to finally let go of the secret dreams she'd been harboring and start working with Jo Wells to finalize the adoption.

For Holly's sake.

She would look at the profile that Jo was bringing with an open mind…and try not to compare the home with the dream home she'd visited with Yevgeny on the weekend.

Then she would have to face up to Yevgeny himself when he collected her tonight, and tell him what she'd decided.

Applause thundered around the theatre.

The dramatic stage curtains came down as the

first act of *Giselle* reached its dramatic conclusion. The lights came up. Around them the audience was already swarming up the aisles to take advantage of the intermission. Yevgeny was in time to catch the transfixed glow on Ella's face, before she blinked rapidly.

"Glad you came?"

Ella shivered. "Good grief, of course! Thank you. It's incredibly powerful."

As Yevgeny got to his feet, Ella gave herself a shake. He could see her starting to come back down to earth.

"How can they possibly top that performance in the second act?" she asked as she rose. Her delicate chiffon wrap dropped from her shoulders, exposing the deep V-shaped back of her fitted black dress.

Yevgeny tucked his arm around her waist and ushered her into the aisle ahead of him. She didn't shake his hand away, so he left it there. Nudged from behind, he pressed up against her, all at once aware of the warm softness of her body against his. His gaze lingered on the soft skin exposed by the dress.

He ached to touch that skin, run a finger down her spine, see the frisson of desire convulse her.

The emotions that had played out on stage in the first act had heightened all his senses. The love. The despair. And the intense passion.

His awareness of Ella leaped higher, blazing through him.

Yevgeny swallowed.

This was truly crazy!

As they emerged from the theater into the lobby he murmured, "Let me fetch us a couple of glasses of wine."

She hesitated, then nodded.

In relief he swung away. Surrounded by the din of chatter, he took a moment to assemble his thoughts, to deal with his fascination for Ella. A waiter bearing a tray filled with tall, slim champagne glasses was coming toward him. Yevgeny took two glasses.

At a touch on his arm, he glanced sideways—and broke into a smile.

"Jerry, how are you?" Then his smile faded as he remembered the gossip. Jerry's wife had left him for another man. Awkwardly he held up the glasses. "Sorry, no free hand to shake yours."

An uncomfortable pause followed, and then Yevgeny caught sight of Ella's blond head on the other side of the room. "Good to see you again, Jerry."

"Call me—perhaps we can play golf sometime," Jerry said.

Yevgeny nodded. "I'll do that." Then he made his way over to Ella and handed her a glass.

After a few minutes the bell signaling the end of intermission sounded.

Ella turned away and handed her still-full flute to a passing waiter.

Yevgeny sensed a black hole opening between them. Widening with every second that passed. Yet he couldn't find the words to bridge it.

What to do? To say? Yevgeny wasn't used to floundering for words. He was decisive. A leader.

He wasn't accustomed to this rudderless uncertainty.

Carefully he inched forward. He rested his fingers on her arm. She jumped. He let her go at once.

"Time to see what the second act holds." Ella threw the comment back over one pale exposed shoulder as she made her way back to the theater. "Let's see what the ghosts of jilted brides intend to do to the lying, faithless Albrecht."

That jolted him back to the present.

What was Ella going to say when she learned about the deception Keira, Dmitri and he had been engaged in?

The baby deserved honesty from all the adults around her. Not just from Ella. Holly was the innocent in this situation. Yet, ultimately she would suffer most from any deception.

Shame smothered him.

Ten

"You've booked a table for dinner?" Inside the confines of the cockpit of the stationary Porsche, Ella stared at Yevgeny in horror.

What to do now? How could she possibly tell him about the couple who wanted to adopt Holly amidst a room full of diners having a wonderful time? How could she kill his hopes in such a public arena?

It seemed too callous.

But if she asked him to take her home, and invited him in for a nightcap back at her town house, the night nanny—and Holly—would be waiting....

They needed somewhere private.

"Aren't you hungry?"

"A little." But she wasn't up to enduring two hours of polite pretense in a high-society restaurant while she sat on new information that involved Holly's adoption.

Maybe she should simply insist he take her home... and wait until tomorrow, then ask him to meet at her office? That would be appropriate. Yet Ella didn't want to leave this any longer—Yevgeny deserved to know of her decision.

Holly.

It was all for Holly.

Her chest ached, and she felt quite ill. Ella knew her heart was breaking. Her glasses had misted up. She couldn't possibly be crying?

Ella ducked her head and fished in her purse for a tissue. Removing her glasses, she gave them a perfunctory polish then put them back on. The mist had cleared.

Yevgeny was watching her.

"Don't you feel like going out? Would you prefer to have something light to eat at my apartment? With a glass of wine? I have a fabulous cellar."

That was a solution, although wine might not be such a good idea—not now that Holly was drinking breast milk.

And Ella discovered she was curious to see where he lived, to find out what lifestyle he would be shedding when he moved into his new home. The next wave of pain washed over her.

Goodness, she was behaving like a goose.

"That sounds like a good idea—but I had a late lunch so don't go to any trouble. I'm not that hungry."

"Hold on." The Porsche growled. They started to nose forward out of the theater's parking lot. "Won't be long now."

Ella pulled out her cell phone to text Holly's night nurse not to wait up for her.

The talk to come might take a while.

Yevgeny's penthouse apartment was perched high above Auckland City like an eagle's nest.

From the private elevator, Ella alighted onto a steel mezzanine bridge spanning the length of the penthouse. Two steps down, and Ella found herself in the living area with Yevgeny right behind her.

Black marble floors gleamed under blindingly bright track-mounted spotlights. The immense space stretched miles to the left and right. In front of her a wall of glass framed the unfolding cityscape like an enormous, dramatic work of art.

"This is awesome."

Yevgeny touched a panel on the wall and music swelled.

One end of the vast living space was filled with a high-tech kitchen dominated by jet-black marble and the brash shine of stainless steel. In the center of the space, a slab of glass suspended on white marble blocks and surrounded with designer ghost chairs gave a highly luminous, yet strangely floating, transparent take on a dinner table. To her left, a sitting area was furnished with sofas constructed of blocks of black and gray leather artfully arranged to take advantage of the view beyond.

"There's no television." Ella was surprised by the absence of electronics.

"Oh, it's here—you just can't see it."

Yevgeny walked to the sitting area and picked up a sleek object that, had Ella given it a second glance, she would've assumed to be a modern artifact. He pointed it at the glass wall in front of the sofas. With a soft click a narrow panel alongside the window slid open. A second click and the largest, slimmest wide-screen television Ella had ever seen rose out of the floor.

The mind boggled. "Very James Bond."

Amusement flashed in Yevgeny's eyes. "The theater sound system has been built into the walls and ceilings." He moved a finger and the television came on. "There are blinds that roll down to block out the light. Then this becomes a home cinema. The security system is also wired in."

The picture on the television changed and the screen split into a grid of images. As her eyes

flicked from one image to the next, Ella could see
the Porsche parked underground, the entrance to the
private elevator where they'd been minutes before,
the concierge desk in the lobby as well as images of
rooms she had not yet seen. A huge bedroom with
a scarlet bed clearly designed to reflect the passion
of the occupant, caused her to glance away.

"There must be cameras everywhere in this
apartment. Don't you ever feel...watched?"

"There are no cameras in the guest washroom."

Ella shot him a wary look to see if he was joking.
His face appeared to be perfectly straight. With
an edge she said, "How very fortunate for your
female...guests."

Yevgeny gave her a lazy smile. "All my guests
deserve a modicum of privacy."

This...this was a playboy's pad, jam-packed with
boy-toys. Ella searched the screen. "What about the
guest bedroom? Any cameras in there?"

"There is no guest bedroom—only the master
bedroom and bathroom—and a study. I'll show you
around if you like."

"The ultimate bachelor's dream," she said, not
ready to acknowledge his offer to show her his
bedroom. Although her heart had picked up at the
thought of standing with Yevgeny in the same space
as that wildly passionate scarlet bed....

Her eyes roamed the living area, seeking a distraction.

Minimalist. Glossy hard surfaces. Hardly the kind of place that a child could visit. It belonged on the pages of interior-design magazines and was far removed from the house Ella had visited with Yevgeny on Sunday.

That place—while big—was meant for a family.

"I see why you wanted to go house hunting," she said.

A pang of guilt stabbed her. Ella knew she was procrastinating. It was time to talk to Yevgeny about Holly's future.

The bubble of hope he'd been fantasizing about was about to burst. And it was an unrealistic fantasy—Ella had only to look at the kind of place he lived in to know that his lifestyle was totally unsuited to a child. Buying that dream house wasn't going to change who Yevgeny was.

Even though she'd discovered he was capable of patience and enormous devotion toward Holly, it was not enough.

He could not provide the family Holly needed.

But, Ella told herself, that didn't mean he could have no relationship with Holly. An open adoption allowed that. They would both be able to be part of Holly's life.

Holly would have it all. A wonderful family and plenty of support from both sides of her biological family. They were all giving Holly the best chance of success in the circumstances.

Yevgeny had opened a panel in the end wall to reveal a bar complete with a fridge below the counter. "Would you like a glass of Merlot? Or I can offer Sauvignon Blanc—or what about a flute of chilled Bollinger?"

About to ask for a glass of mineral water, Ella changed her mind. What the hell, a woman didn't have the chance to drink Bollinger in this kind of place too often in her life. And the effervescence of champagne might clear the sadness that was settling around her like smog at the end of a winter's workday.

With a determined smile, she said, "Bollinger, please."

"Have a seat."

Yevgeny turned back to the bar fridge and extracted a frosted jeroboam. A moment later he popped the cork. Perched on a sofa, Ella listened to the sound of the champagne being poured into two tall flutes and tried to tell herself that everything was working out for the best.

Crossing to where she sat, he handed her a glass, then settled down beside her.

Ella felt her pulse pick up. Partly due to anxiety, she knew, because of the discussion to come about Holly's new family. But there was more to it. Sadness—obviously—because the time with Holly was drawing to an end. And beneath that was another layer: the unsettling edginess that Yevgeny always aroused in her.

She focused on that layer of restlessness. When she'd first met Yevgeny, she'd have identified this feeling as…animosity. Now it had metamorphosized into something else. Still unsettling—but far from unpleasant.

There was excitement…anticipation…and a hint of apprehension, too.

Ella took a small sip of the bubbly liquid then set it down on the highly reflective glass side table. Mistake. Without the drink to focus on, all her awareness centered on Yevgeny.

Her skin prickled and shivers spread through her. *Oh, God.*

She shut her eyes.

The music danced along her senses. Sweet. Pleasurable. Ella tried to focus only on that.

It didn't work…because listening to the music led to thoughts of the ballet earlier…which led her to think about the man who had invited her.

Opening her eyes, she found herself impaled by

Yevgeny's startling stare. Her heart stopped, then resumed with a jolt.

The silence between them had swelled to an expectant readiness.

When Yevgeny reached forward and cupped her face with one hand, her lashes feathered down and Ella sighed softly.

To Yevgeny's astonishment, the hand that cupped Ella's cheek was shaking.

White-hot emotions chased through him. Emotions so intense, so charged, he did not know what they signaled.

All he knew was that it seemed right to kiss Ella.

With great care he removed her glasses and set them down on the table beside them. Then, moving slowly, he leaned forward. His lips closed over hers. He tasted her gasp, and deepened the kiss. Ella gave a husky, raw moan and relaxed back on the sofa.

Desire burned him.

His heart thundered in his ears as he shifted his body across hers on the black leather and slanted his head to seal their mouths together. Beneath him Ella was soft, incredibly feminine. Still cupping her head, he feasted on the lushness of her mouth, devouring her. He could feel her heart thudding against his chest, and he knew she felt the intensity of this as much as he did.

Ending the kiss, he slid his lips down along the skin of her neck, tracing the V neckline of the sexy dress with open-mouthed caresses until he stopped at the hollow between her breasts. He nuzzled at the lilac-scented valley.

Under him, Ella shivered.

And Yevgeny reacted.

His thigh sank between hers, causing her dress to ruche up.

The temptation was too much. He ran one hand along the soft skin of her inner thigh until he found the lace edge of her panties. He eased his fingers beneath the lace. Lifting his head, he watched her as his fingers roamed closer...closer.

Ella was breathing quickly now, in soft, shallow gasps.

He touched her.

She was slick and already wet. Her back arched off the leather, and her eyes closed tight.

It was his turn to moan.

Withdrawing his hand, Yevgeny shifted off the sofa, so that he kneeled beside her.

"Why are you stopping?" she whispered, her eyes still tightly shut.

"You want me to carry on?"

Gold eyes glinted at him through dark lashes. "Yes!"

Sliding his arms beneath her, he hoisted her up and rose to his feet in one smooth move.

Ella grabbed at his shoulders. "What are you doing?"

"Taking you someplace more comfortable," he murmured. Then he bent his head and licked her ear, his tongue exploring the spiral shape. The moan that broke from her this time sounded wild.

In the softly lit bedroom, he let her slide down his body and as soon as her feet found the carpeted floor, he unzipped her dress. He drew her out of the dress and lifted her onto the bed.

He tore off his shirt and trousers in record time. A moment later, clad only in underpants, he joined her on the bed.

Ella was wearing only wisps of black lace.

Against the red satin of his bedcover, with her blond hair and pale skin, and the skimpy bits of black lace, she looked provocatively sensual.

The low-cut cups of her wicked bra revealed curves he hadn't known she possessed. Until now.

He touched the indent of her waist, and traced the flaring outline of her hip. His hand rested on the rounded flesh of her bottom, then he stroked up along the groove of her spine. Her skin was like silk. Just touching her aroused him.

"You are lovely."

For a moment uncertainty glittered in her eyes. "Hardly a supermodel. You've dated—"

"Hush." He placed his index finger on her lips to silence her. "Now there is only you. No one else."

It stunned him how right speaking those words felt.

Only Ella?

But he wasn't ready to consider why it felt so right. Not yet. And not now.

He stroked her stomach where only a few weeks ago a baby had rested. The emotions that flooded him were too complex to name.

All he knew was that somewhere in that cocktail was gratitude. He sank his head down and kissed her belly, paying homage to her fertility and femininity.

Then, slipping a hand under her, he unclipped her bra with a deft flick and brushed the lace aside.

His breath caught.

Ella's breasts were full and high. The dark nipples stood proud. He touched them with reverent fingers. "Are they tender?" he asked.

She shook her head.

His index finger traced a light blue vein beneath the taut, pale skin. This was life. This was the very essence of womanhood—and Ella's nurturing of Holly.

Her hands were on him now, stroking up his chest,

along the apex of his shoulders and down his arms with soft, feathery caresses.

Immediately he became aware of his body's response to her touch. He was hard and quivering. Ella placed a hand on either side of his hips and pushed his underpants down his legs.

As the full aroused length of him was revealed, he heard her breath catch.

He flung his head back.

Her fingers were sure and clever. She touched him in ways that drove him to the end of madness…then summoned him back.

When he could take no more, he fell back on the bed and pulled her with him, the satin smooth against his skin. Pushing off the last remaining bit of lace, he gently eased two trembling fingers into her slick warmth. Her flesh stretched around him. He moved his fingers, fluttering them, seeking the hard nub that made her breath stop.

When her breathing was ragged, her eyes wild, he shifted over her. With great care, he sank into her, then withdrew. Entered again. And pulled away.

Her arms came round his back, and her fingers dug into his buttocks. "Don't go," she pleaded. "Stay with me."

"Show me what you want," he demanded as passion ripped his heart apart.

Ella didn't hesitate. Within minutes she'd torn any control he'd had to shreds. He felt himself going... going...

As Ella's body clenched around him, he felt the first shudder. She arched beneath him, bucking and twisting, and he could no longer hold on as pleasure flooded them both in a torrent of sensation.

"Will you marry me?"

Whatever Ella had expected him to say on opening her eyes this morning, it was not this.

Her mouth dropped open. "M-marry you?"

His face filled her vision as Yevgeny nodded slowly.

She rolled away from him and dropped her legs out over the edge of the bed. Her naked back to him, she pressed the scarlet cover over her bare breasts and scanned the floor frantically for some sort of clothing.

"This proposal is a bit sudden."

Was this the point of the invitation to the ballet... and the romantic restaurant dinner he'd planned afterward? Had the whole evening been nothing but a staged seduction to get her to do what he wanted?

Except a date to the ballet followed by dinner need not have ended up in bed. *She'd* been the one to veto dinner. In all fairness to Yevgeny, he'd only invited her to his penthouse at her prompting. Ella shook her head to clear the confusion and struggled to focus.

Why had he asked her to marry him?

"Why?"

He didn't answer. But she sensed a distance between them that hadn't been there a moment ago.

The idyll had been shattered.

It had been such a beautiful night.... Ella had felt transported. From the moment the ballet had begun the magic had wound itself around her. As though she'd entered a hidden, undiscovered world of possibilities she'd never imagined. As for the night that had followed...

Not once but twice he'd made love to her.

The beauty of it had called to her. That feeling of exploring an intimate link she'd never dared dream existed. A moment of pure, blistering ecstasy. Then freedom. She'd encountered a facet of herself that she had never known—a facet that fitted perfectly, in fairy-tale fashion with—

She shook her head again, her hair whipping around her face.

There was no such thing as fairy tales—she of all people should know that.

Behind her he spoke in a low voice that breached all the barriers she was rebuilding. "Come back to bed."

Oh, she was tempted. To give in, to give up all her tightly held defenses and surrender to pleasure.

To the vision he offered.

"Say yes, Ella. Come lie with me again. Make love. We have time."

That seductive purr…

Then reality snapped in.

He had time. She didn't.

She was supposed to be meeting Jo Wells and the family who hoped to adopt Holly in—she squinted at the clock beside the bed struggling to make out the numbers without her glasses—an hour. And all she had to wear was a skimpy black cocktail dress, which she couldn't even find.

She would also have to explain to the night nurse and to Deb—who would be arriving at her town house by now—why she hadn't come home last night. The round-the-clock care she'd hired for Holly would mean the baby was fine.

But she wasn't.

Ella fought the urge to bury her head in her hands and burst into uncharacteristic tears as shame swamped her.

She'd almost fallen for it— This request to marry her could be nothing more than another ploy to get Holly.

This was not about intimate connections. Or

profound pleasure. Or even about any feeling for her. This was about Yevgeny getting what he wanted in any way possible.

She'd do well to remember that.

Still clutching the covers to her chest, she leaned forward and scanned the carpet. Finally she caught sight of a puddle of black. Her dress. Her bra and briefs were nowhere to be seen. Ella had a distant memory of Yevgeny taking off her glasses last night; she'd have to retrieve them from the living room in order to locate her underwear.

For now she snagged the black dress with the tips of her fingers. In a smooth movement she pulled it over her head and shimmied it over her torso. It seemed absurd to protect her modesty now, but she no longer wanted to be naked in front of Yevgeny. Not until she'd worked out his motives.

Turning her head, she looked at him, fully looked at him, and her heart contracted.

He reclined against the pillows, the sun slanting through the window revealed his lips curved up in a sensual smile, while lazy appreciation still lingered in those glittering wolf eyes.

Lust bolted through her.

She wanted him.

Again.

Even though she suspected his motives.

How *could* she still desire him?

What kind of black magic had he unleashed on her? How had he managed to reduce her to...this? Never had anything interfered with her ability to think...to reason clearly...until now. He had her tied up in knots.

And no doubt he knew it.

It had been his plan.

Suspicion cooled her ardor like a bucket of icy water.

"No."

"No?" He raised a dark brow. "You don't want to stay?"

She flushed. "No—I can't marry you."

Ella emerged from the master bathroom, her purse under her arm. The transformation from siren to icicle was complete. Her makeup was perfect—and no doubt her underwear was back in place, too.

Instead of looking at him where he lounged in the big bed, she pushed her glasses up her nose and glanced down at her watch. "It's late—I have to go."

"Work. I suppose." Yevgeny resisted the urge to roll his eyes skyward.

"My work is important to me." Her voice cooled. Finally she looked at him. "But this time it's about Holly."

He started to pay attention. "Holly?"

Ella was fiddling with pulling the neckline of the black dress straight. He bit back the urge to tell her it was fine. "I intended to tell you about it last night. But I got...distracted." Her chin lifted a notch, signaling that he wouldn't like what was about to follow.

"Yes?"

"Jo Wells found a couple she thinks will be a perfect fit to adopt Holly."

Yevgeny stiffened at that revelation. "*I'm* the perfect fit to adopt Holly," he said unequivocally.

"I saw their profile yesterday. They offer everything I asked for." Ella swept her hair back behind her ear. "I'm meeting them this morning—" She broke off and glanced at her watch again. "In an hour."

Her stubbornness infuriated him. Fixing his gaze on her, he said softly, "I am absolutely committed to adopting Holly."

"It won't work. We've been through this before." She was talking so fast he didn't even try to get a word in. "You're a billionaire playboy. What do you want with a baby? You haven't thought this through. What will you do with a growing girl? How will you provide the mothering model she requires? What do you know about the needs of teenage girls? This feeling of responsibility will pass."

"I will learn. Whatever Holly needs I will provide," he said fiercely. "Whoever adopts her will also have to develop and learn about the needs she has—no one is a perfect parent from the start." He paused for an instant. "Parenting is about committing to learn about the needs of children." Something his own selfish mother had never made any effort to do.

But Ella was already turning away. "I've got to get to this appointment—and I need to stop by my town house to collect some suitable clothes first."

He could not risk Ella allowing a couple to get their hopes up about adopting Holly—he was taking Holly. Nor could he take the chance that Ella would get it into her head to sign the consent to adoption. Twelve days had passed. She could do it now.

"Then I will have to come with you."

She swung around, her face tight and closed—a world away from the woman who had responded so passionately to him last night...all through the night. A tight band settled around his chest.

"I don't want you to come. This is going to be hard enough without you there making it more difficult for me."

Yevgeny got out of the bed. Ella recoiled. Impatiently he reached for a pair of jeans slung over the blanket box at the end of the bed and dragged them on. Buttoning the fly, he said, "My intention is not to make it more difficult—but to make it easier—"

"You're not doing that!"

"Ella, you should consider my proposal—"

"No!" She warded off his reaching hands. "No. No. *No.* I'm not marrying you!"

He wished she would stop interrupting him, stop rejecting him and stop pushing him away. She was making it so much more difficult…for both of them.

"Ella. *Listen to me.* I am Holly's father."

Eleven

"*What?*"

Ella's eyes stretched wide with shock. Finally, anger set in.

"What kind of stunt is this?" He'd tried persuasion, coercion—all with no luck. So last night he'd taken her to bed and, while she still basked in the warm, golden glow of his lovemaking, he'd asked her to marry him. *Now this.* Ella marched toward the bedroom door. "I don't believe you."

His hand closed around her arm.

"Wait!"

Fury broke over her. She yanked her arm loose. "Don't touch me!"

He put his hands up in a gesture of surrender.

"This is no stunt. I am Holly's biological father…I donated the sperm."

Frantically Ella searched his face, seeking something—anything—that would prove his claim a lie. Instead, she saw only calm, unwavering certainty.

Her shoulders sagged.

Holly's father. Not her uncle…

The dizzying discovery changed everything. And explained so much.

Like exactly why he'd slept with her last night. And why he'd asked her to marry him…and why he just refused to give up in his pursuit to adopt Holly.

A heavy weight sank over Ella, until it settled deep in her belly. He wanted Holly so badly—because she was his daughter.

The queasy feeling in Ella's stomach grew. Churned. Nausea rolled over her in turbulent, battering waves.

Vivid images flashed through her mind. Yevgeny demanding to know where the baby was that first day in the hospital. Yevgeny bending over Holly's cot, entranced. Yevgeny producing Nadiya as his fiancée so Holly would have the mother Ella demanded. Yevgeny's fury whenever she'd tried to roadblock his efforts. And the picture that hurt most of all? Yevgeny kissing her…loving her…to get want he most wanted.…

Holly.

The next realization struck her.

Yevgeny wasn't going to give up. Ever. Last night's seduction had already proved just how far he would go to get Holly.

As Holly's biological father, he would be eligible to adopt the baby. The prohibition against a single man adopting a girl child did not apply to a father.

Ella's lawyerly brain went into overdrive. Hell, he might already be contemplating the first step: applying for guardianship. Ella knew she could challenge that. After all, Yevgeny had not been married to her—or even in a relationship with her. But there was a chance that a judge would grant the order because Holly's best interests were a stake. Once he'd been appointed joint guardian along with her, Ella suspected he'd waste no time seeking temporary custody of the baby. He was Holly's biological father; the court might look favorably on it. Unless she fought him. When Holly had been born, Ella would have done anything she could to stop Yevgeny getting the baby.

But now?

Ella bit her lip. He loved Holly. How could she stand in his way?

There would be some formalities to go through—paternity tests—not that Ella doubted that what he'd said was the truth. She could hear it in his voice, see it in his eyes. He was Holly's father. Even the hard-nosed, skeptical-lawyer part of her believed it. The court would, of course, demand incontrovertible evidence. But Ella knew the tests would prove beyond doubt he was Holly's father.

And once he'd secured temporary care of Holly he'd launch a formal application to adopt the baby.

"You're going to use the courts to get Holly," she breathed.

"This is not—"

"You're not going to give up, are you? Why didn't you tell me this before?"

"I hoped to convince you without having to reveal this."

"You're ashamed of being Holly's father?" But that didn't make sense.

His eyes caught fire. "Never!"

"Of being involved in sperm donation?"

"I'm not ashamed of that—but to be honest, I don't think my grandmother would have been too keen on the idea." He shrugged. "But with her recent death that's not relevant anymore. If Keira and Dmitri had adopted the baby as planned no one else need ever have known the truth."

"Not me." Ella made it a statement. "And not even the person who needed most in the world to know the truth—Holly."

"Of course I knew Holly would have to know one day. Ella—"

She warded him off with blank, blind eyes. "But when Keira and Dmitri decided they didn't want Holly—why didn't you tell me then?" An instant pulsed past.

He took two long steps closer to her, and when she shuddered, he halted. "I was as shocked by the situation as you were. The first day I couldn't think straight." He'd expected Ella to do the motherly thing and keep the baby. But he didn't want to say that now. He wasn't prepared to risk extinguishing the burgeoning understanding that was forming between them. "We were always at such loggerheads. And I couldn't tell you…immediately."

"So when did you intend to tell me?"

By the time it had sunk in that he'd have to tell her, Keira and Dmitri had already flown off to Africa. In his arrogance, he'd believed Ella would be grateful for his offer to take the baby from her unwilling arms; he'd never expected her feisty resistance to his proposition. Well, he'd sure discovered how mistaken he was.

"Once I'd spoken to my brother—"

Ella laughed, a high, hopeless sound that sounded wild and desperate, cutting off his clumsy attempt at an explanation. "Sure. Now you need your brother's permission? You've never waited for anyone else in your life before you act, Yevgeny. Now you want me to believe you needed your brother's permission?"

Strangely enough he could understand her pain, her anger. She'd stood so firm in her conviction to be transparent, to do the very best for Holly. To the point where she was prepared to keep in touch with the baby as she grew older so that Holly would have a fully developed sense of her own identity.

"And why you? Why not Dmitri's sperm?"

The first wave of shock had passed. He could see her brain starting to process the information. "I'm trying to explain."

"Then get on with it."

God, this was hard. Even though he now knew how it must hurt her, Ella had been determined to be honest with the baby to whom she'd given birth.

He'd been less honorable.

Regret ate at him. But he couldn't change his actions, couldn't make them more honest. All he could do was explain what had driven his deception. And be totally honest in his relationship with Holly from now on. "Ella, you need to understand…"

Ella focused on him and the pain in her eyes caused the words to trail away and his heart to clench. Then she raised her eyebrows in a way that brought his feisty Ella back. "*I* need to understand?"

He had to make her understand. "I needed to clear it with Dmitri—because it involves him."

"Does it? I'd say that the essence of the situation is that it doesn't involve him—he played no part in Holly's conception." She dropped her head into her hands. "And all the time I thought—" Ella broke off and lifted her face. "Keira lied to me, then—she was part of it."

Ella had gone white.

Yevgeny started toward her, but stopped when she glared at him.

"Keira had no choice," he told her. "Dmitri didn't want anyone to know—although he disputes that now."

"I don't believe that she kept this…this…from me. I'm her sister—I offered to carry the baby she wanted. She owed me some loyalty…she *and* Dmitri." Her mouth twisted in a rictus of a smile. "Or perhaps Dmitri never wanted a baby—and he was just stringing Keira along."

"That's not true!"

"Isn't it? Then why the elaborate charade?"

"Because my brother is sterile!" he announced.

There was a deathly silence.

Then Ella said, "Oh." After a moment she said, "But why such a big secret? Everyone knew from the outset Keira couldn't have babies. There was no big secret about that."

"It seems that it is my fault."

That got her attention. "Your fault?"

He sighed and rubbed a hand over his hair. "Yes."

"Was there an…accident?" she asked carefully.

It took Yevgeny a moment to realize that she'd taken him literally. "I didn't cause my brother's sterility," he said broodingly. "But apparently I caused him to be ashamed of his lack of manhood."

Ella stared at him without responding.

He laughed without humor. "So it would appear you are right. I am the big-brother bully. My brother didn't want anyone to know because he feared I would be angry—while I thought he didn't want anyone to know because he would feel…awkward."

"You were trying to protect him."

Yevgeny shrugged. "Except he doesn't see it that way."

"Of course he doesn't. He only sees it from his side—because that's what you've allowed him to do all his life. You've allowed him to be selfish. You created a monster."

He opened his mouth to object to the attack on his brother.

But Ella was already speaking. "Don't worry—I've done the same thing." She lifted her hands and shrugged. "I've indulged Keira so much that she doesn't need to take responsibility for anything. She simply needs to dump it on me and swan off secure in the knowledge that I will take care of it." Ella hitched her purse up. "Whatever 'it' happens to be at the moment."

"And right now it is Holly."

"Exactly."

It took a minute of silence for that to sink in. Yevgeny found himself smiling at her as a newfound sense of truce surrounded them. "We're a fine pair, aren't we?"

Ella glanced at her watch. "Good grief, the meeting. I need to fly."

"I am coming with you—don't even try to keep me away."

Ella was relieved that today was over.

Jo Wells had dropped her home. Ella had been extremely grateful. She had a headache and it had taken all her energy to persuade Yevgeny that she didn't want him taking her home. She needed nothing more than to sleep—which she'd done, while Deb had tended to Holly.

Now she sat curled up in the rocking chair in Holly's nursery, watching the baby sleep in her cot while the night nurse took a coffee break in the kitchen.

This morning's meeting had been unspeakably difficult, despite the fact that Yevgeny had behaved like a saint. And, to make things worse, Jo Wells had been right.

The family was delightful—everything Ella had once wanted for Holly.

Holly. It was all about Holly.

Only Holly.

Too soon Holly would be gone....

Ella knew she shouldn't be thinking about herself. About how she was going to feel once Holly had gone. But she couldn't help herself.

She'd taken all possible precautions to stop this from happening yet still it had happened. She'd grown attached to the baby lying in the cot only feet away.

One thing had become clear to Ella—Yevgeny wanted to adopt the baby with his whole heart. He might not be listed on the birth certificate as Holly's father, but she didn't need to have blood tests run to confirm his paternity claim. She believed him—even though the lawyerly side of her would force her to cross the *t*'s. His desire to keep Holly wasn't a spur-of-the-moment whim driven by impulse. He loved Holly—he was her father. Holly was his daughter, a part of him.

An ache filled Ella. Holly was a part of her, too. Her daughter.

Their daughter.

Her heart was telling her Holly belonged with the father who already loved her...even though he was far from perfect.

Could she forget about the plans—dreams—she'd had for Holly to go to the perfect family? And give Yevgeny what all his billions would never buy him?

That way there would be no messy, turbulent court battles...no legacy of bitterness.

Ella rose to her feet and went to stand by the cot. Inside Holly slept peacefully.

"What do you want, my angel?" she asked the baby.

It was Christmas Eve.

Using the excuse that his brother and her sister were both away in Africa, Ella had invited Yevgeny around for dinner. She hadn't been surprised when he'd leaped at the opportunity to spend time with Holly.

Ella had decorated the table with cheery green-and-red place settings for her and Yevgeny. There was a place for Holly, too, and Ella planned to draw her stroller up to the table for dinner to participate in the event.

This Christmas Eve was special.

It was Holly's first Christmas Eve. And, Ella knew, it would be the only Christmas she would ever spend with the baby. At the moment the baby was lying on her back on the carpet wearing a cute Santa's elf outfit.

She looked absolutely adorable.

Ella had spent the afternoon since returning from work taking photos. One day Holly would be able to look back through the album that Ella would put together for this day. In fact, Ella had decided to keep a duplicate copy of the album for herself...to form an invisible bond between her and Holly.

Forever.

A secret they would share.

The doorbell interrupted her musings.

That would be Yevgeny.

Opening the door, she found him standing outside in the warmth of the evening sunshine, his arms piled high with goodies and gifts.

"You shouldn't have." She laughed, ushering him in. "Put the presents under the tree. Actually, let me help unpack the top items first."

There was a bouquet of flowers, chocolates, an iced Christmas cake...and crackers.

"This wasn't necessary," she scolded.

"What? And deprive me of the opportunity to spoil Holly rotten?" He started to pack the gaily wrapped parcels under the tree. Ella couldn't help noticing how well his black jeans fit his narrow waist and long legs, and how the T-shirt clung to his muscular shoulders.

Oh, my. All he needed was a red bow and some ribbon to be someone's perfect Christmas present.

But she had to remember he wasn't intended for her.

She swallowed. "Can I get you something to drink?"

"There's a bottle of red wine somewhere in here. Or it may still be in my car— I'll go check."

"I'll find it," Ella said. "Look, here it is."

But Yevgeny had already disappeared through the front door. He returned minutes later without the wine—but this time he carried an enormous boxed gift as tall as he was.

Ella did a double take. "What is that?"

"A playhouse—one to set up inside, until I get the one in the tree built."

Ella couldn't help herself. She laughed.

They had eaten dinner. Lazy now, Ella sat on the carpet in the living room leaning against the sofa, her legs stretched out in front of her with Holly cradled in the crook of her arm sucking sleepily at the last dregs of her bottle, while Yevgeny sprawled in front of the Christmas tree with his head propped up on his elbow, watching them both through pale, wolf eyes.

"Holly is almost asleep," Ella said softly, bending her head.

The baby was heavy and relaxed in her arms.

For so long Ella had been at pains not to hold or feed Holly, to keep her distance. Yet tonight she was eager for the experience. With Deb gone home to enjoy Christmas with her family it seemed like the right time. Ella knew that she was going to spend plenty of time with Holly over the next two days, and that she'd grow fonder of the baby with every hour, making the final wrench of separation so much harder. But she'd accepted that.

With the pain came immense pleasure. The joy in watching Holly's mouth twitch as she sucked. The satisfaction of stroking a finger along the baby's velvety skin. And these precious days would give her a chance to say goodbye to the baby.

But tonight there were three of them—herself, Yevgeny and the baby.

Almost a family.

To escape that delinquent thought she glanced

back at Yevgeny, and asked, "What was your first Christmas memory?"

The flickering red-and-green lights on the tree reflected in Yevgeny's colorless eyes.

"The Christmas season would run from the last day of December to around the tenth of January. When I was a boy, on New Year's Day we would hold hands and form a chain around the tree and call out for Grandfather Frost—not Santa Claus. He would hand out presents helped by his granddaughter, the Snow Maiden. There were always tables laden with food, a total contrast to the food shortages that my parents had grown up with. Things denied us during the rest of the year appeared. A goose. Cakes. Meatballs. Pineapple— My mother queued for hours to get pineapple. I'd almost forgotten about that. And no celebration would be complete without *kutya*."

"*Kutya?*"

"A kind of porridge made from wheat berries, honey, poppyseed and nuts. My *babushka* would make it a few days in advance because that way, she used to say, the flavors had time to develop. But the best part, the part I couldn't wait for, was watching my grandmother hurl a spoonful of *kutya* up at the ceiling in the hope that it would stick."

Ella found herself laughing. "She sounds like a character."

"Everyone did it—it was a tradition. The theory went that if the *kutya* stayed stuck to the ceiling, a successful honey harvest would follow. And that is good for everyone—because honey represents happiness and success." His mouth softened into a smile, and even the hard angles of his cheekbones disappeared as he lost himself in the memories.

"Your grandmother must've been a wonderful woman."

"Oh, she could be a tartar, too." He reached out and grasped the hand resting on Holly's cheek. His fingers tightened around hers. "But she made Christmas special."

Who would make Holly's Christmas special?

The sudden question flitted through Ella's mind with the speed of light, causing her to stare down at the little angel in her arms. Not her—she wouldn't be around to be Holly's mother. Yevgeny had a wealth of tradition that she would never have expected. But where would the mother figure in Holly's life be?

Yes, she would visit—but would that be enough? Ella shook her head, her throat tight. Why was she worrying? Yevgeny loved the baby, and he'd clearly forged a strong bond with Holly. What did it matter that Holly would have no mother figure? She would have a father who loved her.

"Ella?"

She looked up.

"What are you thinking?" he asked softly.

The tightness in her throat made it impossible for her to speak. She shook her head instead.

"You love her, don't you?"

She hesitated, then nodded. It was true. Holly had crept into her heart against Ella's will and twisted herself around it. She bit her lip, struggling to hold back the tears that threatened.

"You've come to a decision," he prompted.

The tears spilled over. She nodded. Only once. Then her face puckered up. Ella knew she was going to disgrace herself by sobbing all over Yevgeny.

She found her voice. "I think I'll take her upstairs and put her to bed."

His hands clenched hers. "You're running away."

"No!" She simply wanted to get herself under control. Ella rose to her feet, and his hand slipped away. "I won't be long. I'll be back in a few minutes."

When Ella came back to the living room, Yevgeny's gaze fastened to her. He'd settled himself on the sofa, and she hesitated a moment before perching on the opposite end. She turned so that she was facing him, and drew her bare feet up onto the seat.

"You've decided you're going to keep the baby," he said.

Ella blinked at him. There was loneliness in his eyes. Was he giving up? "No, I haven't changed my mind." At least not about that.

"No?"

This was so hard. "I love Holly."

There, she'd said it. Now for the next bit...

"But my keeping Holly would not be in her best interests." Ella got restlessly to her feet.

"Because you've got your mind fixed on wanting her to be raised by a family?"

Because she'd make a terrible parent. "That's part of it, but not the only reason I can't do it."

She'd reached the Christmas tree. Ella leaned forward and scooped up a wrapped scroll.

"I'd planned to give you this tomorrow, on Christmas Day. But now is as good a time as any."

She handed it to him. He took it with reluctance. "Open it," she said.

He drew out the document she'd rolled up and secured with gold ribbon. "What is this?"

Even as he pulled the ribbon loose, Yevgeny stared across at Ella.

She sighed. "It's my consent to the adoption."

He glanced down. "Why give it to me..."

The moment his voice trailed away Ella knew he'd seen his name. "It's in your favor."

When he looked up, the brilliance in his eyes made her want to cry. But this time with joy…and relief.

She was doing the right thing.

"I can't offer her a big sister—or a mother," he said. "But I can offer her a home, a garden, a place to call her own."

"I think Holly will be very fortunate to call the house we looked at together home."

"But more than a home, I can offer her every bit of love I am capable of giving. And I can offer her an aunt and an uncle—" he hesitated "—and a tummy mummy who are all her family."

The sweetness of his words caused her to smile.

"What about the other family?" he asked.

His concern caused her heart to melt. "I've already told Jo—she promised to let them know." At least she'd never told them they were getting the baby. To hold out hope then snatch it away in such circumstances was more than Ella could bear.

Mixed up with a sense of sadness at the goodbyes she needed to say to Holly once Christmas was over was relief that Yevgeny wouldn't be taking her away. He wouldn't whisk Holly away to Russia—or London. He would be working and living in Auckland. He was buying a house with Holly in mind. She'd seen the room that would be Holly's. She would be able to visualize Holly safe in her

home, keep her in mind in the months—years—
that lay ahead.

Ella knew she would see the baby and, thanks to
Jo Wells, Yevgeny knew how important it was to
her that this be an open adoption.

She shouldn't be feeling like this....

So empty.

Like her guts—her heart—had been ripped out.

Get over it. For once, Ella found the bracing words
didn't work.

So she tried reason instead. Her daughter would
still live in the same city, not across the ocean in
another world.

And she would stay in touch with the baby.

That made Ella feel better.

While Holly would not call her mom, she would
always be Holly's tummy mummy—Yevgeny had
made that clear. She felt a lump forming at the back
of her throat. The alternative, cutting all ties to the
little girl, would be so much worse. It was not an
option—not for Holly.

And not for her.

Yet the night he'd made love to her, Yevgeny had
offered more. He'd asked her to marry him. She had
said no in a way that had brooked no argument. For
one wild, magic moment Ella considered what might
have happened if she'd accepted.

Then she shrugged it away. The moment was past. He would not ask again. Why should he? He had what he wanted....

Holly.

Why would he want her? He didn't even like her....

Why could it not have been different?

She quickly stifled that thought. That would mean that she never agreed to act as surrogate for Keira and Dmitri, that Holly had never been born, that she would never have gotten to know Yevgeny better.

And those were things she could not contemplate living without now.

Because she loved Holly.

As for Yevgeny...she was so confused about the swings of emotion he aroused in her. Anger. Passion. Empathy. And something she feared to name.

So when his arms came around her, the lighted Christmas tree, the gaily colored packages, all dissolved in a blur of tears as Ella started to weep uncontrollably.

Twelve

"Hey, don't cry," Yevgeny whispered against Ella's hair, and his arms tightened around her.

She snuffled. "I'm not crying." And she felt him smile.

"Sure you're not." He pressed a kiss to the top of her head. After a moment he added, "Thank you for my Christmas gift. It is without a doubt the best present I've ever received."

"My pleasure." Ella found she meant it. With her tears stanched, she lifted her head and warned him, "But you better make Holly happy."

His expression deadly serious, he said, "My offer is still open. If you marry me and come live with us, you'll be able to gauge for yourself how happy she is."

Ella's heart leaped, and then settled into a rapid beat.

The offer was unbearably tempting. Looking away, she focused on the flickering of the Christmas lights. There was something about the powerful emotions that Yevgeny stirred in her that made her suspect she was falling in love with him. Heck, not falling… fallen.

She was in love.

It had been so long, she'd forgotten how it felt to be in love.

And back then it had been so different. Young love. This time it was deeper…less impulsive. Yet Ella knew if she accepted Yevgeny's proposal she needed to be sure that her love was strong enough for both of them. There could be no going back because Holly would suffer.

Of course, they shared that bond. She loved Holly…and Yevgeny loved the baby, too.

But, despite his proposal, Ella was under no illusion that he loved her. He never had. Could he learn to love her in the future? Was it worth taking a chance on that? Could she love enough for two?

"So what do you think?" he asked at last.

"I'm scared," she said honestly, switching her gaze back to find him still watching her with that unnerving intensity.

"Scared? *You?*" There was disbelief in his voice. "But why?"

Not ready to confess that she wasn't sure about the wisdom of going into a marriage where he didn't love her, she said instead, "I don't know that I'd make a very good mother."

He reared back and looked down at her. "What makes you think that? You're wonderful with Holly. I didn't think that at the start but you've managed to convince me. Your love for her is evident every time you look at her."

"My parents haven't provided the best template, but to be truthful, that's not the only reason I think I'd be a hopeless failure as a mother…and wife."

"Who was he?"

She gave him a startled look. "How did—" Ella broke off. Then, "What makes you think there was a man?" she hedged.

"Your reaction." Yevgeny's brow was creased in a frown of concern, and his hold loosened, giving her more space. "Tell me who he was."

Did she really want to expose herself to the possibility that he might not even understand her pain? Perhaps the time had come to reveal something more. It was the only way to discover if there was substance to this attraction that floated between them.

Her shoulders slumping, she said, "I was eighteen, he was nineteen. We were in love."

A shadow passed across his face.

"You can't imagine it, can you?" Ella pulled a face. "I was besotted. I thought it was forever."

"What happened?"

"I got pregnant."

He sighed, the sound overloud in the living room of Ella's town house. Something cold shriveled in Ella's chest. "It was perfectly predictable," she said. "He disappeared as soon as I told him. All his promises of our future together vanished as he ran for the plane to take him to a new job and new future in Australia. Within weeks I heard he had a new girlfriend, too."

"And you were left holding the baby." Ella could feel the tension that coiled through his body even before he asked, "You had an abortion?"

She gave him a sharp look and broke out of his arms, shifting to sit on the side of the sofa farthest from him. "No!"

"So what happened to the baby?"

"The baby," she said through stiff lips, "died."

This time Yevgeny brooked no resistance as he took Ella in his arms.

Her body was rigid and she felt worryingly cold.

He rubbed his hands along her arms, and marveled that he'd ever considered Ella a human icicle.

She was complex, yet kind. And she'd endured more than any woman should need to.

"I'm sorry."

He brushed his lips over hers in a gesture of sympathy. Her mouth clung to his, and Yevgeny kept the contact until she finally broke it.

"Thank you."

He let the silence surround them, not pressing her to tell him more. It was curiously companionable, with no rough edges as she nestled closer. His hands stroked along her back, touching, offering wordless comfort, even as Yevgeny wished he could take the pain from her.

When she did speak, she lifted her face up to him and said, "Make love to me."

"Now?" His hands paused in their stroking. "Are you sure?"

She nodded, her honey-colored eyes pleading. "Yes. Now. Here. I want to feel alive again."

This time their loving held a well of tenderness.

Rather than passion, it was care and concern that Yevgeny expressed with every stroke and touch. Only when her body softened, became increasingly fluid, did he finally pull her over him and let her take him into her.

Then he rocked her.

Slowly and so gently. Until the sensations built to a peak and the passion broke.

When it was over, he pulled her up against him, and held her tight.

A while later, Ella straightened up. "I feel much better." She sounded surprised. "Definitely more alive."

"Good."

She sat up slowly and reached for the clothing she'd discarded. "You've been very patient."

"It's one of my less well-known qualities." He gave her a small smile and was relieved when her eyes sparkled back. After she'd pulled the garments on, Yevgeny reached out his hand and took hers. "I'm here for as long as you need me."

Astonishment flitted across her face, followed by acceptance. "Thank you."

"I'm the one who needs to say thank you," he said, "for giving me Holly."

"The other baby—" Ella broke off.

"You don't need to talk about that if you don't wish to."

"I want to." Her eyes met his bravely. "The other baby was going to be adopted out. It was a closed adoption—my parents thought it would be for the best. I never knew anything about the family she was going to—only that they couldn't have children.

Once the baby was gone…I knew I would never see it again."

That's why she'd been so insistent about an open adoption this time around, he realized. "That must have been hard to deal with."

Her eyes had gone blank. She'd retreated into the world of the past. "The morning I went into labor—I changed my mind. I wanted to keep the baby. My parents wouldn't hear of it. We were still fighting when I went into labor. It was a boy."

Yevgeny waited. Nothing he could say would be adequate to comfort her.

"But something went wrong. The cord was wrapped around his neck…and he died. I felt like I'd killed him—by changing my mind and deciding to keep him."

"No!"

"I know. It's not a rational fear. But it took me a long time to come to terms with it."

Yevgeny finally understood why it had been so difficult for her to change her decision to give Holly up to a couple who could love her…to give her to him.

It had taken courage. She'd had to conquer her demons.

"You're the bravest woman I've ever met," he told her.

It was then that he realized how deeply he loved

her. But now was not the time to convince her that marrying him would heal them all.

So all he said was, "Come, let me hold you."

When the doorbell rang on Christmas morning, Ella had no idea who could be outside.

She pulled open the door to find Keira and Dmitri on the doorstep, luggage piled up beside them. "You're back!"

Concern instantly settled over her. What had gone wrong? Then she gathered her scattered thoughts.

"Merry Christmas! Don't stand out on the doorstep. Come in."

Ushering the pair into her living room, while leaving the luggage stacked in the hall, Ella asked, "What happened? Why've you left Malawi?"

Keira came to a halt in the middle of the room and exchanged glances with Dmitri.

"Ella, we've changed our minds."

Something in her sister's tense tone caused adrenaline to surge through Ella's veins. "You've changed your mind? About volunteering in Malawi?"

But she knew...

It was much, much more.

"No, about the baby." Keira's words confirmed what Ella had already sensed. Keira wore a mulish expression. "Dmitri and I have decided we're going to keep Jessica."

"Jessica?" Ella's brain was spinning. "Her name isn't Jessica, it's Holly."

"We've chosen to name her Jessica." Dmitri placed an arm around Keira's shoulders and drew her close.

This was what she'd wanted…wasn't it? Taking in their unified pose, Ella swallowed. She'd hoped for Keira to change her mind and keep the baby. Yet now confronted by the pair who had just announced that's what they wanted, Ella found the idea of losing Holly terrified her.

Then anger set in.

"But you gave her up—you told me to sort everything out."

"We made a mistake."

Her sister's eyes filled with tears. For the first time ever, Keira's tears failed to move Ella. The customary protectiveness failed to materialize. This time it was Holly she wanted to protect.

"You decided you weren't ready for a baby yet."

"That's what we thought, but the time in Malawi made us decide we're ready for parenthood."

"It's too late, Keira—"

"She's already been adopted? You've signed the consent?" Keira must've seen the answer in her eyes. "You should've let me know—"

"You walked away—you made her my problem. Remember?"

"Because I knew you would be able to give her up for adoption—you've done it before. And you did it without any trouble." Keira huddled closer to Dmitri. "I'm not as tough as you, Ella, I couldn't face the pain. I could never have done it."

Tough? A shaft of pain shot through Ella. Was that how her sister saw her? Did no one see how painful these decisions were for her? Ella swallowed. She'd lost one baby—she wasn't losing this one. "I couldn't give Holly up."

"Then why did you imply she's been adopted?"

"Wait, let me get a word in edgewise. I never said she's been given up for adoption. I'm getting married—I'm going to keep her."

"Married?" Keira gave a laugh of surprise. "To who?"

"Your sister is marrying me."

The dark voice came from behind her. Yevgeny. Relief swarmed through Ella as he enfolded her in his arms. She shut her eyes and allowed herself to lean into his strength.

Strength. Comfort. Understanding. That was what he'd offered her through this period of turmoil. He'd been there for her—and Holly—every minute. He'd never failed her or walked away.

He was a man in a million.

A man worth loving. Forever.

It would be so easy to abdicate all responsibility, to let Yevgeny take over. But it wasn't fair.

Ella forced herself to keep steady. And to think. Was this the best course for Holly? She loved Yevgeny but he didn't love her. But he was reliable. He would never leave her.... She knew from what he'd told her about his mother walking out on him and Dmitri he would never do that to his own child. Could she marry him under such circumstances, knowing there was no way out?

"We came back for the baby." Dmitri stood toe to toe with his older brother.

"Until you change your mind again next week?"

"We won't."

"Ella and I are hardly convinced. Until you turned up here today we haven't received one call from the pair of you to find out how the baby was."

"I called," objected Keira. "Only once but at least I called."

"This is true?" Yevgeny spoke into Ella's ear.

She nodded slowly, and waited for him to stiffen, to release his hold and withdraw his support.

But he stayed exactly where he was.

Before she could say anything, Keira started to speak. "Yes, Ella told me she'd hired a nanny, that she was back at work. I felt so guilty. I knew the baby was screwing up her life."

Ella closed her eyes. "Things changed."

She'd changed.

And Yevgeny had noticed the change even as she'd started becoming aware of it herself. She thought back to their visit to that magical house...the day he'd kissed her for the first time.

Ella placed her hands on his forearms, emphasizing their unity in the face of her sister and his brother. What they were doing was right. They both loved Holly.

They would make this work.

It had to.

Her resolve hardened. "I'm sorry, Keira. I got pregnant for you originally. Then you and Dmitri decided you both needed time and space for yourselves. But now I can't give her up. I'm her mother."

Saying those words freed something deep inside her. All the hurt of the past softened, eased and floated gently away.

For the first time in many years, Ella felt...whole. At peace.

"After my first baby died, I thought I'd never smile again..." Her voice trailed away.

Behind her the rise and fall of Yevgeny's chest slowed. His arms tensed into bands of steel around her.

Keira's face crumpled. "None of us could reach you."

"I'm happy now. Holly has brought me happiness. Please be happy for me— I don't want to fight you on this," she said to her sister.

There'd been enough fighting. Against Yevgeny. Against herself. But she would fight no longer.

"Keira, I haven't discussed this with Yevgeny, but why don't we talk about you and Dmitri becoming Holly's godparents? That way, you can both have a significant part in her life." When Keira's eyes brightened, Ella started to think about the old saying that it took a village to raise a child. Holly would never be short of family. She glanced from Keira to Dmitri and finally to Yevgeny. "What do you all think?"

Yevgeny nodded, his expression unfathomable.

"We'll discuss it," said Keira. "But first I want to be matron of honor at your wedding."

Ella knew she should come clean and reveal there might be no wedding—she hadn't yet given Yevgeny his answer, even though she'd told Keira and Dmitri they were getting married.

Ironically, she now desperately wanted to marry Yevgeny—but there was still a stumbling block.

He didn't love her.

Thirteen

Red. Yellow. Green.

The Christmas tree lights lit up Ella's pale face.

Holly was having her afternoon nap, and they'd finally seen Keira and Dmitri off after they'd stayed for Christmas lunch. Yevgeny had given the pair the keys to the Porsche and the freedom to stay in his penthouse. He would've done anything to get rid of them.

Because he needed to talk to Ella.

She'd announced to his brother and her sister that they were getting married—that she was keeping Holly. He should be pumped…everything he wanted was falling into place. But he didn't like the quiet air that had settled around her like a shroud. It was a far cry from the happiness expected of a bride-to-be.

"Ella, are you okay?"

Her hands paused in the act of picking up the shredded wrapping paper that lay on the carpet, left over from the orgy of unwrapping that had taken place earlier. Holly had gotten a treasure trove of gifts. The eyes that looked up at him held confusion—with none of the honey-gold tones that indicated happiness. She pushed her glasses up her nose in the way she had when she was uncertain.

"Do you think I've been too hasty?" she asked. "Holly was born for Keira and Dmitri—should I give her back to them?" The pain in her eyes was blinding. "It would give Keira the gift of happiness I intended all along."

"But what about you?"

She stared at him. "Me?"

"Yes, *you.*" This lay at the heart of the matter, he realized. He came to stand in front of her. "What do *you* want?" Ella blinked up at him. "I think, for once in your life, you need to think about what you want. And go after it."

The bewilderment faded, and a strange expression came over her face. Her eyes flicked to him, then shot away. "That would be selfish."

"You deserve to be happy, too."

"It's not just about me. There are other issues at stake here, too."

He placed his finger under her chin and tilted it so that he could see her eyes. They were guarded. "Like what?"

"Like you."

He tried to read her, started to hope. "What do you mean?"

"I don't want you to feel obliged to marry me because of what my stupid pride caused me to say to Keira."

Had it been pride that had caused her declaration? He'd thought there'd been a lot of honesty—her love for Holly had shone from her.

Yet now doubt shadowed her face.

"You're having second thoughts about giving Holly up?"

She shook her head. "No, she belongs with you."

"You could belong with us, too. If you choose." His finger trailed along her jawline and stroked her hair off her face as he'd seen her do so often in the past. He was no longer sure whether marriage for Holly's sake alone would be enough for him.

In the past few weeks his fears had changed. He no longer dreaded that Ella would abandon Holly someday, as his mother had abandoned his father, himself and his brother. He now feared that she would never be able to love him. Hell, she hadn't liked him that long ago. His own arrogance had cemented that. At least the raw antagonism had diminished. He could make her laugh. He was certain she at least liked him now.

But love?

Not yet.

He didn't want to wait for her to fall in love with him—to live in uncertainty about whether it would come to pass even as he took her to his bed each night.

He wanted her love. Now.

But he didn't want to put more pressure on her, either. This time he had to be selfless, this time he was putting Ella first.

This was about Ella. It was her choice.

"What do you want, Ella? What is your dream?"

Ella bit her lip.

How to tell Yevgeny that her dream lay at the magical home he'd bought for him and Holly. She wanted to share that home with him and Holly—she wanted to share their future.

Because she loved them both…more than anything in the world. Between the two of them, they'd taught her to love again. They'd brought her back to life.

Yevgeny's hands cupped her face.

She met his gaze…and trembled inside.

Could she risk revealing her dream to him? What if he ridiculed it? Or dismissed it? As quickly as they came the thoughts vanished. Once they'd come to an understanding about Holly, Yevgeny had shown her nothing but kindness. And passion. *That* thought swept in from nowhere and caused her cheeks to heat.

"Let me tell you what I never dared dream of." His voice broke into her thoughts. "I never dared dream that I'd one day have a family. You see, my family was a train wreck. My mother and father had a dysfunctional relationship and when my mother left, she used me and Dmitri to get what she wanted— financial support while she swanned around with her new lover."

Ella knew she should have suspected something like this; all the clues had been there. She should have worked out that he was the childhood victim of a bitter divorce.

"Your mother got custody of you both?" she asked slowly.

He nodded, his eyes vulnerable. "She took us away from Russia—to London. Until she decided she wanted to be young and unfettered again and ran off with her toyboy. My father came to fetch us— it was the first time we'd seen him in three years. She'd fed the court a bunch of lies, and he'd been barred from seeing us."

"I'm sorry," she said, and took a step forward.

She wrapped her arms around this strong man, and leaned into him. She kissed his cheek.

He dropped his face into the cleft formed by her neck and shoulder, and said so softly that she had to strain her ears to hear, "I never wanted to marry—to risk that happening to my child. I was not ever going to give any woman that kind of power over me."

Ella struggled to absorb what he was telling her. But he'd asked her to marry him. What did that mean? Was this regret for flouting his vow to himself?

Probably.

Ella knew exactly what to do. She had to set him free. Dropping her arms, she said, "And now I've gone and told both our families that we're getting married. I'll tell Keira it was a mistake."

"No!" He raised his head. The expression in his eyes caused her breath to catch in disbelief. "Ella, you don't understand—I *want* to marry you. That's the dream I never dared to dream. I love you."

To Ella's horror, she felt tears prick.

"Hey, I didn't mean to make you cry."

That caused her to smile through the tears. "I'm sorry. I don't normally cry this much. But these are tears of relief—and joy. You see, I love you, too."

At that, Yevgeny's arms encircled her and crushed her to his heart.

* * *

"Are you happy?"

"Me?" Ella turned her head to smile at her fiancé. Yevgeny's arm rested around her waist as they stood on the wide veranda of their dream home taking in the view they'd be seeing every day in the new year. "I'm walking on clouds—life couldn't be better."

The sale of the house had gone through. In a few days they would be moving in.

Everything in her world was going right.

Ella glanced down at the stroller beside them, where Holly was quite comfortably ensconced. For now. In years to come Ella knew Holly would tear around the gardens, explore the trees…and play on the swing Yevgeny intended to build. Perhaps there would be a younger sister. Maybe a brother, too.

A hand cupped her chin. Instantly her pulse quickened. Yevgeny bent his head and sealed her smiling lips with a kiss.

When he raised his head, she said, "Did you ever imagine this could happen between us?"

"I'll tell you a secret."

She tipped her head back, waiting for him to continue. "Yes?"

"I used to think you were an icicle. I didn't think the man had been born who could melt you."

"No secret." She laughed. "I knew what you

thought of me. But you once told me you never could resist a dare. Was that how you viewed me? A challenge to defrost?"

"It never crossed my mind. I have to say that I must be incredibly blind because you're the warmest, most passionate woman I've ever known." He ran a finger over her bottom lip. "You're not angry?"

"I'd be hypocritical if I was." Ella paused, then grinned. "You see, I thought you were a bully—I called you Bossy Big Brother."

"I'm not a bully!"

"Ah, but I thought you were. I thought you controlled every aspect of your brother's life, and that was why the poor thing was so irresponsible."

Yevgeny swung round and leaned against the balustrade. Placing his hands on her hips, he drew her closer. "What can I say? I admit it. I did pull him out of too many scrapes."

"I did the same with Keira. It was easier to sort her mistakes out for her than let her learn to do it herself." She grinned at him as she allowed her body to rest against his. "At least we won't make those mistakes with Holly."

"I have no doubt there will be others to make."

Ella looked up at him, aghast. "Good grief. I hope not."

"But don't worry. Like her mother, I know she's ticklish—under her feet."

"How long have you known that?"

He paused. "I'll tell you something else I know."

"What's that?"

"The night I discovered Holly was ticklish, I overheard your promise to our daughter that you'd find her the best mother in the world. If you ask me, I think you've done that."

Her heart stopped. "That's the nicest thing you've ever said to me."

"And it's perfectly true. Come here my wife-to-be. Let me show you again how much I love you."

This time when his mouth closed over hers, he was in no hurry to end the kiss.

* * * * *